STRONG FEATHER

The Story of the Last Covey in Indian Bend Wash

By Richard Inglis Hopper

Strong Feather
by Richard Inglis Hopper

Printed in the United States of America

ISBN 1-60034-462-3

www.xulonpress.com

DEDICATION

Dedicated to quail watchers everywhere.

CONTENTS

ACKNOWLEDGEMENTS

I am grateful to the members of my family for their encouragement and many ways they helped this book come together. I also want to thank Bonnie Thompson for her valuable insights and helpful suggestions.

CHAPTER ONE

"Mommy," a little voice complained, "this is not my favorite thing."

With a craning neck and questing eye down the trail, the mother comforted: "It won't be long. We have to be patient."

It was just after first light and a large crowd had abruptly stopped on the path. The complaining child and its mother were in the midst of much chatter and many clucks interrupted only by searches for a snack—pecking at a speck here or stripping a leaf there.

The little one lunged hungrily at a yellow butterfly, bit and immediately spat it out with a "Bleah!"

"Oh, child!" his mother scolded. "What are you doing?"

"Ugh! Tastes awful!"

"Of course! The yellow butterfly is poison! You should know better."

"But I'm so hungry!"

Another mother watched and clucked sympathetically. Then, as much to the complaining little one as to others nearby, "We have to wait for Grandpa-Q."

"Yes," another mother agreed. "He will know what to do."

"I wish he would hurry. My children are so hungry and it's getting so hot."

"You can't hurry him. He has his work to do." "He seems to be taking longer than ever."

Another mother crowded into the shade of a summer-weary plant. "All this complaining is enough to set your feathers on edge. Nowadays children don't know what it's like to miss a meal or suffer even a little bit."

"What's taking him so long?" a neighbor groaned. "It's so hot already! I've got to get my children to water."

"It didn't cool off a bit last night. How long can this go on?"

"Honestly, I've never seen it so hot for so long." An anxious searching look down the trail. "Now where is that man?"

The press of the women and children pushed the men off to the side, where they were glad to be out of the confusion. The constant scratching and pecking on the dry soil raised puffs of dust that caught the slant of the early sun. The men sniffed at the dust, shook their heads at the complaining, and tried to ignore the noise as they talked among themselves.

"What do you make of it?" Old Quaymon asked no one in particular.

Quyor answered: "I'm not sure. Grandpa-Q will have the answer. "

"Yes. He will know what it means and what to do."

"Maybe so. Before he makes some big announcement, I'd like him to talk it over with us this time."

Soon everyone had a comment.

"Maybe that's because he knows about things—like what Mr. Sun tells him—that we have no way of knowing."

"Even so, we are supposed to be in charge of things."

"Yes, but I wonder what happened down there and what it means. It sounds like trouble."

"Sounds? That's the problem. There are no sounds this morning."

"You know what I mean."

"Hmmph."

"I've got some ideas about what we should do," one said. Another put in, "Yes, so have I. Some ideas we should talk about."

"If we are in charge, what are we waiting for? Let's go!"

"Wait a minute, now. We don't want to do anything we might be sorry for. He can't be much longer, can he?"

"Everything he does seems to take longer and longer."

"Don't complain. You know why."

"Yes, of course, the Memory Stick. I hate to say it, but Grandpa-Q is getting on."

Uncle-Q, who had come from across the water, said quietly, "Let's see what happens." He raised his head and squinted at the sky. "Good start for another hot day."

"Don't worry. I know he's working on it."

"It's certainly taking him a long time."

"He says he wants to be sure."

A mother called a caution to children who were restlessly running and playing up and down the trail. "Come back, you! You know better than to run off!" She glanced around anxiously. "Shouldn't someone be up on the fence this morning?"

"Those men!" a mother nearby said. "They just stand around and talk —mostly about the weather—and forget their responsibilities."

"Yes, we need someone. Even here."

"Especially here. Why just the other day, I saw Cat prowling around—"

"And Hawk—" An anxious glance at the sky. Hawk was circling, but so far away that there was no immediate danger. "Always there, just waiting—"

The children ran back. "He's coming!" they shouted. "He's coming!"

Their calls brought the crowd to fluttery concentration. Rounding the bend down the trail, the one they were watching for came toward them.

"Aren't they fine-looking?" Grandma-Q asked.

"Yes, Mama-Q said. "Don't you think that Grandpa seems tired this time?"

Grandma-Q laughed. "I was about to say that Grandpa looks better this morning. You're right. It has been hard on him."

Down the trail, Grandpa-Q and Papa-Q walked slowly, chatting and browsing.

"You seem encouraged this morning," Papa-Q said.

"Finally, we have good news. I think we have a better grip on things now."

"Even without the Memory Stick?"

"Yes. People talk about the Memory Stick, but I'm not so sure it had what we need. The fire, you know."

"It has been more difficult, hasn't it?" Papa said, "I mean, without the knowing of the old stone. Why don't we work out something new and go on from there? So you won't have to go through this again."

"Yes. It is something to consider, but very carefully."

"If we did it now, we'd have your marks—" Papa-Q stopped. "I don't mean to say."

"I understand. People say I'm getting on. There's no need to do anything like that. You will be here to carry on."

Up the trail, the waiting crowd was restive. One of the mothers shook her head impatiently. "Just look at him! Lollygagging along!"

"You'd never think there was anything to worry about!" another complained. "Just taking his sweet time."

"Give him a chance," Uncle-Q said. "They've been working while you were sleeping. How could he know what's going on?"

"He knows," Aunt-Q said. "Of course he knows."

One of the children shouted with excitement: "Come on! Let's walk with him!"

Little-Q and Cousin-Q and others ran down to greet Grandpa and escort him.

Down the trail, Grandpa pounced on a particularly succulent morsel and, as he lifted his head, saw the children running toward him and, behind the children, the crowd waiting.

Shrill voices, full of excitement called out: "Come on, Grandpa!"

"Hurry, Papa!"

"We're all waiting for you!"

The two men and their young escorts came up to the waiting crowd. Suddenly everyone was talking at once.

Grandpa shook off a moment of confusion, and turned to Papa-Q. "Isn't this wonderful? They've all come to hear the news."

He smoothed his feathers and hopped up to a patch of higher ground beside the trail.

The low rays of the new morning sun flashed across the land and reflected off his topknop. He stood tall now, his action transforming him from a lollygagging grandfather to the leader of the covey.

He had not seen so many in such a state so early in the morning. Why, everyone was here. There was a mood of anxious restlessness. Sort of a hunger, it seemed to him. Truly, this was most unusual.

He was so full of his own news that he thought that somehow the people sensed it and came to greet him and hear his announcement.

"A beautiful morning!" he said. "Yes, beautiful!" He appeared especially happy. The crowd quieted and listened. "I have good news!"

All at once, a deep silence of anticipation. He was pleased that they would honor him in this way in his old age. As a child, he had seen the people honor his grandfather, and wondered if such a thing could ever come to him. Now it was happening. Perhaps, he thought as he looked over the covey families, these youngsters were developing some reverence for the old ways, the old values. Even without the handing down of the knowing of the Memory Stick.

Deep in his feathers, he sensed that this was probably his last year with this news. Next year, his son would be making this announcement. He glanced at Papa-Q with a sudden sadness for himself, yet a pride that the traditions of their people would be carried on into the future.

"Mr. Sun," he began. He stopped, overcome with emotion. He took a deep breath and tried again: "Mr. Sun—"

A rustle of restless movement swept over his listeners.

"Mr. Sun —" He sensed that this was not what they expected to hear. He paused, listening. He started over: "Mr. Sun—"

He was interrupted by a voice with an impatient edge. "We don't care about Mr. Sun today."

Another voice: "No. We've had enough of Mr. Sun."

Another: "Never mind that. What about the horses?"

"Yes! And what about breakfast?"

"My children are hungry. May we go to breakfast now?"

The shouts took Grandpa-Q completely by surprise.

"The horses? Breakfast?"

After a long silence, he repeated, "Breakfast?"

"Yes, breakfast," a hungry voice came back. "No one has had breakfast, waiting on you—"

"I don't understand," he said, shaking his head a little, a move which vibrated his topknot. Everyone began talking at once. Two words came through again and again: "Horses!" and "Breakfast!"

Grandpa-Q sank back, flabbergasted. He glanced at Grandma-Q and said something. Although his words couldn't be heard she understood him: "All this fuss and the question is—breakfast?"

Lowering his head and turning it this way and that so he seemed to hear first one side and then another, Grandpa-Q nodded gravely. "Yes, yes," he said, and turned to the next one.

The crowd ran out of breath and words. Grandpa-Q looked over at one of the elders, and his head tilted slightly in a question, as if to say, "Tell me, if you can, what is this all about?"

The elder, Uncle-Q, came up and said, "Don't you hear it?"

The crowd became quiet, watching Grandpa.

There was the noise of the cars and trucks on the road, a sound which was so constant it formed the background to their lives and was no longer noticed. In the intervals between waves of traffic, the soft flow of water in the canal as it passed the weir. A mockingbird and grackle quarreling in a treetop in the distance.

Not a sound from the crowd. Hardly anyone breathed. A little one giggled at the sudden silence and was hushed.

Finally, Grandpa said, "I don't hear anything."

Everyone breathed at once and another elder shouted, "Exactly! Precisely! No-body hears anything!" He separated the words emphatically.

"Because they're gone," someone said.

"Gone?" Grandpa asked. "Who? What?"

"The horses!"

Papa-Q, who learned the news from the people around him, and wanting to be helpful, stepped forward. "Yes. The horses are gone."

At this, a bluster of words rose up from the crowd like a wave and fell back to silence.

"The horses?" Grandpa asked. "Gone? Are you sure? They might be out somewhere, like they do."

"We've only looked from here," Uncle-Q said. "We didn't know if we should go near. If something is wrong."

"Yes, it doesn't sound right," a mother said. "I'm sure something is wrong and I'm not sending my children up there without knowing what's going on."

The crowd became noisy, calling out questions and opinions, mostly about breakfast and hungry children.

Grandpa and three of the elders moved to put their heads together, but Papa-Q interrupted. "Enough talk. Let's go see about it."

"Yes!" someone called. "You go scout it out."

"And," another added, "come back and tell us."

"Good idea," came from a third, "but make it quick."

Papa-Q looked questioningly at Grandpa-Q and, instinctively, both cocked their heads, listening intently. They looked up at the sky, around and above the crowd. They scanned the horizon.

"Why don't you see what you can from here," Grandpa said, indicating a fence post.

"Yes, good idea," Papa-Q said. He quickly swept up to the top of the post. Again, he listened, looked, scanned.

Little-Q gazed up at him, his eyes full of the vision of a covey leader standing alert and ready, his body and topknot outlined against the broad blue of the morning sky. Guarding the covey, guarding his family, guarding him. Seeing his father like that spoke to Little-Q deep inside. He felt it, but did not understand it.

Papa-Q dropped to the ground and nodded. "Looks all right." Grandpa said quietly, "Be careful. No telling what's going on down there."

Papa-Q began moving cautiously down the path beside the fence line, which the covey used as their trail to the stables and the browsing ground. His action brought calls of encouragement from the crowd.

Grandpa-Q hushed them. "Let's not stir things up and make trouble for him."

Papa-Q turned and waved, then was out of sight around the bend in the trail.

As the crowd watched him go, Grandpa said, "Let's just wait quietly together, then."

Everyone became still. This stillness was not as it was when a frightened mother would give the alarm signal. That would freeze her children and everyone else within calling distance. Now, adult and young waited cautiously for any sound from the stables and corral. Hopefully, it would be an "all clear" signal.

If alarmed, they knew that Papa-Q might fly quickly and noisily in a direction away from the covey to protect those waiting. Or he might limp helplessly away from the trouble-spot, to lure the danger in the wrong direction. Or, like others in his clan, he could remain very still, making himself almost invisible until it was safe to move again.

The quiet, coming after all the noise and confusion, was almost comforting. The air was warm, even hot for those in the sun. It was uncomfortable to be without breakfast for so long. Yet they waited.

Uncle-Q went up to Grandpa-Q and whispered, "What's taking so long?"

Uncle-Q got a scowl from Grandpa for breaking into his concentrated listening for Papa-Q.

"With the work, I mean," Uncle-Q whispered.

Grandpa, irritated by this interruption, spoke out loud: "You know good and well why. I have nothing to work with."

A cry sounded from the stables and carried down the trail to the covey. Instantly alert, every topknot was turned toward the call.

They saw Papa-Q standing tall on a fence post, silhouetted against the sky. His head high, he repeated his call: "All clear!"

The crowd glanced at Grandpa-Q, as if asking permission to go. The instincts of the covey seemed to hold, at least temporarily, above the hunger of a late breakfast.

Grandpa raised his wings expansively. "Yes! Let's eat!" he said loudly.

Everyone ran in a rush down the trail toward the stables. Once there, they scattered over the corral and into the stalls and around the grain bins. For now, the place belonged to the covey and everyone took full advantage of it. The area was taken over by a ground cover of bobbing heads and lifting tails.

They worked at eating so frantically that they soon overcame their first hunger and little by little relaxed and took time to look around and talk.

"What happened?"

"Where are they?"

A sage voice filled in the answer: "It's simple enough. They have made their winter move. They left us their feeding grounds."

"Of course!" one answered. "They have moved to their winter home."

Another objected: "Isn't it too early for that? Grandpa hasn't said anything about the cold. He knows— "Yes, I' a third put in. "We are still in the long hot and plenty more to come. Why go now?"

"Any sensible being would get out of this heat," was the answer. "Probably moved to where it's not hot."

"Maybe that's something we should do."

"We have responsibilities."

"Yes, all year round. More's the pity."

A mother looked up. "Don't talk that way," she scolded. "Where would the world be if it weren't for us and Grandpa's work?"

"Anyway they are gone. Good riddance. I worried so much about my children getting trampled."

"Yes! Now we have the whole place without them stomping around and getting in our way!"

"Let's enjoy!"

After a time, the covey ate its fill and the tempo of activity slowed.

Mothers began preening their children.

Some of the young people splashed in the trickle of drainage from the water trough. The older ones preferred the old way of bathing on the ground in a circle of dust.

The elders and other men talked among themselves.

All but old Quaymon, who watched the youngsters splash in the water and impulsively ran to join in. For a few wild moments he reveled in the water, ignoring the stares of the oldsters.

"Old Quayrnon—crazy old Quaymon," one onlooker remarked, "always doing something crazy. When you least expect it."

"Look at him!, another said. "No respect for the old ways." "He always did have a wild streak."

Quaymon ran out of the water, shaking off the last drops. "Why not," he said. "It's a lot cooler the way the kids do it."

After a time, Grandpa-Q went to the stump and hopped up onto it. His appearance there meant something important was going to be said. The people quickly gathered around. Now they would hear; everything would be explained. .

"I didn't have a chance to tell you my news," Grandpa began. The group settled down to listen. This was surely a special occasion and they expected a special announcement.

Mama-Q nudged Papa-Q. "Your father looks tired," she said. He nodded. "Yes. It's been very hard on him this time."

She shook her head slowly. "I wonder how long he can keep it up."

Someone nearby turned and said: "Listen! Grandpa is going to tell us what is going on."

21

On the stump, Grandpa was saying, "...after many awak-enings, Mr. Sun has given us a new message, which we were able to mark..."

He gave an apologetic aside to the elders standing nearby: "At least I believe this is right. I cannot be precisely sure without the knowing of the old stone."

A murmur of expectancy rippled across the group.

"Today," Grandpa said triumphantly, "just look!"

He pointed to the eastern sky, where he saw something that the others did not perceive. He attempted an explana-tion: "He has agreed to turn back. To end this long hot..."

A faint rustle of reaction. Everyone was filled with food and comfortable. The mystery of the horses was forgotten.

There was a long silence after Grandpa's voice trailed off. He stopped his momentous announcement. He sensed that no one was paying much attention.

Aunt-Q, the first to understand the meaning of his words, spoke up:

"You mean, that it's really over? Why, that's the best news we've heard in a long time!" She looked around, searching for a response, for some support for the covey leader, who'd worked toward this moment for so long.

Someone near her grumbled, "I don't feel any different."

Grandpa overlooked the objection and acknowledged Aunt-Q's encouragement.

"Yes," he said, "he is going back, at least for a while, I believe. There will be a little more of this, but the Great Stone tells me that the worst is over for us."

Papa-Q stepped out and hopped onto the stump beside Grandpa. "This calls for a celebration!"

Grandpa looked startled, remembering something important.

"Yes! That's it! I forgot to announce that it is time for the festival!"

The people began to stir with anticipation and a glimmer of excitement. Feathers rustled.

"The festival?"

"Yes! The festival!"

Uncle-Q fluttered onto the stump to join Grandpa and Papa-Q.

"Yes!" he called. "Let the festival begin!"

"No! No!" Papa-Q shouted. "Not yet! Mr. Sun will give us the time."

"Your father said."

"Grandpa said it was the time for the festival, but he didn't say to begin yet. There's a big difference."

"Yes, of course," Uncle said. "The Tall Pole will say." Grandpa-Q said to Papa-Q: "It's your time to go, son. You are ready, I'm sure."

"Yes, and proud to."

"With Little-Q, of course," Grandpa added.

"Yes. Little-Q. If I can drag him away from his play."

"Before you go," Grandpa said, "tell me—what was your first impression when you scouted the area?"

"Frankly, I didn't like it. It was too quiet. Too empty. It put the feathers on the back of my neck up. Then, as I looked around, and found everything just as we left it yesterday— except for the horses—it was rather pleasant. They must have flown away during the dark."

"In the dark time? How could that be?"

"We have seen the Duck people do that."

"Yes, yes," Grandpa said. "Perhaps so."

As they talked, the news took root in the covey, and plans were being made about the dances, the games, the songs, the food.

"With the horses gone," someone shouted, "we can make this really special!"

"Yes! The very best ever!"

When the three men came off the stump, the other elders came to them.

"I don't remember agreeing to this at all," Quyor said. Quanute cut in: "Maybe not, but it's still a good idea. We haven't had any fun around here since—I can't remember when."

"He's right, Quyor," Papa said. "It's time we did something like this, if only to break the hot."

"All right, then. If you all say so."

"Don't worry, Quyor," Quanute said. "Our people need to celebrate. It's been a long hot for all of us."

"If it's a celebration," Quyor said, "why does Grandpa look so serious?"

Grandpa shook his head thoughtfully. "The matter of the horses has me worried. It's just not the normal course of events at all."

He looked at the men standing with him. Making sure he had their attention, Grandpa-Q went on:

"This event with the horses may be nothing, or—" he paused to emphasize his next words—"or it may be more serious than we suppose. Let's take a good look around and see what we can see. Be alert. But we must be careful that we don't frighten the women and children."

CHAPTER 2

Little-Q followed Papa-Q down the trail to the land at the eastern sky where the Tall Pole was a sentinel welcoming Mr. Sun. Papa went straight to the pole, which stood on the high point of a clearing within a circle of sage and wildflowers, weeds and tall grass.

"It will soon be time," Papa-Q said. "Let's be sure everything is ready."

Little-Q stayed with Papa-Q as he moved carefully around the pole and the Great Stone at its base.

"Be careful not to disturb these marks," Papa-Q said. He leaned over a little, pointing. "Watch carefully, now. You must learn the proper way so that you can do it when your time comes and" he looked up, smiling— "and you can pass it along to your son."

A large butterfly flew by. Papa-Q ignored it, concentrating on the work. But the quick fluttering distracted Little-Q. This butterfly was not the yellow poison kind, but a colorful succulent snack. He followed with his eyes, turning his head to watch the large wings move in the air. He was sure the butterfly was teasing him personally, challenging him. It was as if Butterfly said, "Catch me if you can."

Papa-Q went on with his explanation: "Now you will really have to pay attention..."

He looked around. "Do you see — ? Little-Q?"

Papa was surprised that Little-Q was not at his side, looking over his shoulder and observing every detail. Papa-Q raised up and turned to see that Little-Q was some distance away, running toward the plants that grew beyond the circle of the Tall Pole and its Great Stone.

Little-Q had been lured away by the fluttering of the delicate wings. He followed the butterfly, almost as a game, and ran out of sight into the growth of brush and weeds and grass.

Papa-Q called: "Little-Q?"

Little-Q did not answer. He was busy with his butterfly, pursuing it in a playful way, jumping at it now and again, but missing and following it to the next plant. Neither he nor Papa noticed the sleek, silent glide of a large bird that soared in a searching circle above them.

Papa called again, more loudly, with irritation close to anger: "Little-Q! What are you doing?"

Little-Q recognized the edge in his father's voice. He started to run back to the Tall Pole. A shadow crossed over him. It made him shiver.

Papa was so intent on his task at the Pole, and Little-Q so distracted by his game with the butterfly, that neither had been alert to what was overhead.

Little-Q stopped and looked up. It was Hawk. Little-Q watched the graceful shape, darkly outlined against the sky, circle slowly above them. Hawk's flying looked so effortless that Little-Q stared in admiration, innocently wishing that perhaps someday he could fly like that, gliding easily and gently on the wind.

Just spread your wings and glide. Float on the breeze. Look around and decide what you want for your next meal.

The shadow crossed him again, and a chill went through him. He saw Hawk circling closer to the Tall Pole, then suddenly curve into a diving swoop, claws outstretched.

"Papa! Papa!" Little-Q called frantically. "Papa! Look out!" He began to run toward Papa-Q, calling as loudly as he could.

Hawk noticed this new movement on the ground. Hawk swerved, centered on the new target, the running shape of Little-Q. This would be easier to take because it was away from the hazard of the pole. Hawk changed his direction toward the smaller, safer target.

Little-Q felt the shadow of Hawk on his back and knew that now he was the object of Hawk's deadly dive. Little-Q skittered left, right, left, moving as fast as he could. There, off to the left, a large tumbleweed. Big enough to get under. That would give him cover. He raced for the protection of the large round weed.

He crashed into it and pushed himself under the dried brittle branches, not feeling the scratches of the sharp-pointed bristles. He kept going into the center of the protective cover. He made himself small, breathing hard. He was full of terror and sudden shame for putting Papa-Q in danger.

"Oh, Papa! Papa!" he cried. "I'm sorry! I'm sorry!"

For the longest time he could ever remember, Little-Q remained frozen. His heart thumped in his chest. He breathed in frantic gasps. Fear and shame soaked his feathers to the very tips. He dare not move, dare not turn his head to look, even to open his eyes.

After an eternity, he heard Papa-Q call softly: "All clear!"

Papa's voice! Could it be! Little-Q opened his eyes, turned his head. He saw only the bristly branches of the tumbleweed. Papa's call came again.

Little-Q moved carefully to the edge of the sheltering weed and peeked out. The world looked normal. He looked up—no Hawk in the air. Papa called once more.

Little-Q came out from under the plant and saw Papa-Q at the Tall Pole. Little-Q ran to him.

As Little-Q came across the clear ground, Papa called encouragement: "What a hero! You saved my life!"

Little-Q ran to him. Papa-Q wrapped him in a deep hug.

"No, I didn't," Little-Q said. He managed to look up at Papa. "I should have been here instead of playing around. I'm sorry."

"Sorry! You made Hawk look away in the middle of his dive. I had no place to go. He was coming right at me. I was out in the open, and you made him change at the last second. What a move! Are you all right?"

Little-Q nodded.

"I was really scared. Oh, Papa! I'm sorry."

"I was scared for you. But what you did—that was brave!" They huddled together a few moments; then Papa turned back to the Pole and the Great Stone.

"Look! It's time!" he said. "You give the signal."

"Me? I couldn't do that."

"All you do is fly up there on the signal post and give the festival call."

"The post is too tall, and I'm too small."

"Of course you can do it. After what you did, you can do anything."

Hesitantly, Little-Q raised his wings, made a running start, flapping hard. He fell far short.

"Papa," he moaned, "I can't do that."

"I'm sure you can. Listen—you're my son and Grandpa's grandson and you just outfoxed Hawk. I'm sure you can do it. Try again. Harder."

Little-Q tried again, fell short. He was persuaded to try one more time. Papa said: "You can do it! You've got the stuff of heroes!"

On the third try, Little-Q tried harder than he had ever tried anything before, and made it to the top of the signal post. Once there, he looked surprised, but soon got used to it. He felt as if he had spent the morning atop the post. The world looked so different from up here!

Head up, Little-Q made the festival call.

"Good," Papa said. "Again. Louder this time."

Little-Q took a deep breath and called again, pushing it out for all he was worth. He heard a voice down the trail take up the call and pass it on. Step by step, his call echoed down to the corral, where a kick-up of dust told him it had been received and the festival was beginning.

Little-Q and Papa-Q started down the path back to the stables and corral.

"Papa," Little-Q confided, "I don't feel like a hero."

"That's all right," Papa said. "You didn't do it to look or feel heroic. That's always for someone else to say. And I say your coming to help me was something heroic. You had a close call, and so did I."

"It was a dumb thing to do to chase that butterfly allover. I think people will laugh at me when they hear that part."

"All right. We'll keep that between ourselves."

The festival was grand and noisy and raised bursts of dust from the hot dry dirt of the corral. The covey members moved about with a freedom which they never had under the big horses and their giant hooves.

Old Quaymon demonstrated the strutting-booming-puffing of distant relatives on the northern prairies. He performed dances he had learned from a third or fourth cousin when he was very young. Grandpa and others joined in and they taught the children some of the steps.

Aunt-Q sang. Not the usual daily covey calls, but songs that reminded them of the old days and covey members who had been lost. After a time, the children drifted away and began to play their own games.

As Aunt-Q's song ended, the people moved into the shade. A solemn mood hung over the festival.

Someone forced a cheerful: "Boy oh boy! This reminds me of the old days."

"Better!" another answered. "All the food and water you want and no one to trample allover you..."

"You're right! We've never had it this good!"

"I wonder how long it will last," Aunt-Q said in a worried tone.

"Auntie, you're always worrying, " a voice objected.

"She's right," Mama-Q said. "I'm not sure we have deserved so much. So much that it might be taken away."

"Yes," Aunt-Q said. "Things just don't seem right."

"No matter what you think," someone said, "the horses are nothing to worry about. I think it's a good thing."

"Maybe it's a sign, and we should do something about it. I would like to have the Memory Stick so we could see if this has happened before and what they did about it."

"Whatever happened to the Memory Stick?"

"No one has seen it since we moved to this place," Aunt-Q said. "Isn't that right, Grandpa?"

Grandpa said that perhaps the Memory Stick was lost in the wash, when the covey people came to the horses' place.

"Left behind in the excitement, II he said. "Everything was lost in the flood. My grandfather said it was the worst thing he'd ever seen."

"Maybe it's time, then, to make a new Memory Stick," someone suggested.

"Wouldn't be the same without the old stories," Aunt-Q said.

"Grandpa remembers them. He can tell the stories and someone could write them down."

"You can't use any old common piece of wood. The Memory Stick was special."

"Yes. Very, very special," Grandpa said softly. "I remember my grandfather telling about it. It was all the

30

wisdom of the generations. He said that when he held it, just so, it sang to him."

The conversation fell away. After a time, the men drifted off toward the stables. The women watched the children playing.

"Just look at those kids. Not a worry in the world."

"Oh-oh," someone said as Little-Q approached. "Here's one with a worry."

Little-Q ran up to his mother, complaining that Sparrow had ruined the game for him.

"When I go and hide, that bird tells where I am," he cried. "It's just not fair!"

Mama-Q spoke to him quietly. "That's not a grown-up way to act, is it? Crying over a little game? You can talk to him like a grown-up."

Little-Q calmed down. He said he would try. He walked away, slowly at first, then more quickly as he thought about his mother's advice. Soon he was running.

Mama-Q watched him thoughtfully and said, "Perhaps if I'd given him lots of brothers and sisters he would be more used to the give and take of playing games. More prepared to deal with life's little problems."

Grandma-Q spoke up to reassure her: "You can't blame yourself for his being alone in the nest."

Aunt-Q added: "He's at that difficult time between being a baby and being grown-up."

"One of these days," Grandma went on, "you'll see a big difference in him. Probably just overnight, he will be your young man instead of your little boy."

The women watched Little-Q as he crossed the corral.

"His father was like that, " Grandma said. "All of a sudden, one day —"

Mama-Q stifled a sob: "He's so—so—"

"You seem to know something," Grandma said.

Aunt-Q broke in: "What have you seen that tells you—?"

Mama-Q did not answer, holding her thoughts privately, as Little-Q disappeared into the weedy growth beyond the corral fence.

Little-Q ran into the field which lay fallow between the corral and the dry ditch which bordered the road.

Sparrow was taking a dust bath.

"Hey, there!" Little-Q scolded. "You shouldn't give me away when we're playing a game! You nearly spoiled the whole thing for me."

Sparrow moved about in the circle he had made in the earth and shook more dust through his wings. "Really, young man, I did not mean to spoil your game. I was trying to tell *you* that Cat was lurking."

"Cat!" Little-Q was surprised and a little fearful that he had been so busy he had not seen Cat. "I didn't know. "

"Of course you didn't know. Anyone could see that." Sparrow went on with his bath. "We have to stick together in this world, don't we?"

"Thanks, Sparrow. I'm sorry I said what I did. Mama says I'm getting too big for that baby stuff."

"No big deal." Sparrow hopped away from his bath and let a final squiggle of dust run down his back. "But tell me, what's all the excitement this morning?"

"Grandpa talked to Mr. Sun and he agreed to end the hot, so we started our festival."

Sparrow was skeptical. "He did, did he?"

"The horses moved and left the whole place to us," Little-Q said.

"Moved?"

"Yes, you know, made their winter move. Because Grandpa says the cold is coming."

Sparrow said that he had never heard of horses doing that and suggested that they had gone for the day. "Like they do."

The two found shade under a brushy plant and talked about I what had happened.

"I'm sure I heard someone say 'winter move.'" Little-Q insisted.

"Strange things are happening all over this neighborhood. There's hardly anything that would surprise me anymore. Some creatures do move, I guess. Move away for a season, I mean. We haven't done anything like that since—I can't remember when."

"We neither. Not that I know of."

Sparrow laughed: "You know, it has been so hot for so long, maybe we should have made a summer move." He scratched at the dry dirt. "I don't see how you stand it, living on the ground. At least living the way we do, higher up, you know, we get some breeze once in a while."

"The hot will be gone real soon. You'll see. My Papa said so. Grandpa has talked with Mr. Sun a long time and before him his grandfather did and—"

"Honestly, you people have some of the strangest ideas! Talk to Mr. Sun! Next you'll be telling me—"

"I just know that a lot depends on Grandpa."

"I hope he's made a good connection. It's been a long, long hot, and I can't see that it's over. I've got to fly."

He stopped at the edge of the shade. "By the way, I wouldn't go too far north today. Something has been going on up there."

"Maybe there's a festival up there, too," Little-Q said.

"Didn't look like much of a celebration to me." Sparrow hopped out into the sun and flew away.

Little-Q had lost interest in the games he had been playing with the others and browsed among the weeds for a snack.

Grandpa-Q and the elders and the other men found a shady place between the stables and watering trough. It was cooler near the water. Quyor, having eaten his fill and feeling good all around, thanked Grandpa-Q for his work.

"For the past several days," he said, "anyone could see that the situation was in doubt, what with Mr. Sun giving us so much hot for so long. You pulled us through."

"Yes," said Quanute, "it could have gone either way. You've done a great thing, but it seems to me that it's taken a lot out of you this time."

"If it weren't for you, Grandpa," Papa-Q put in, "we could be having more hot, instead of heading into the cold."

Grandpa sent a shrug rippling through his feathers. "I do what I can. I just hope that the situation here will not interfere with my work."

"What do you mean?" Papa-Q asked. "The horses? They've come and gone before."

"Yes, now and again," Grandpa said. "But not all at once. I've looked around. Horses and everything else — gone!"

"It is unusual. Something we haven't seen before."

Grandpa shook his head thoughtfully. "It could be a sign of something even more unusual to come, something that could affect our lives here drastically."

"You mean we would go, too, like the horses?" Papa asked.

"I didn't want to say that," Grandpa said. "But, yes."

"But we don't do like they did," Uncle objected. "Not any more."

"Perhaps this is the time we should think about it."

"At least discuss it," Quanute said sharply.

"Boy, are you guys on a downer!" Quyor said. "Just look around. Everything you could want is right here — and you're talking about chucking it all."

"Life has been so good for us here, it may have spoiled us for anywhere else," Old Quaymon said. "It's not like the old days, when we could just make do wherever we were. I'm afraid we've let the children go soft in this place."

"Yes. It's been too easy for them." "For us, too."

"Yes," Grandpa said. "Too far from the old ways."

"But your work, Grandpa?" Papa-Q asked. "You're not getting too tired?"

"No, no. It's going well. In fact, I'm reaching a critical stage."

"Perhaps I can help."

"I just hope there's time," Grandpa said seriously.

Quyor interrupted: "Don't worry, you two! Everything's going to be all right. You'll see."

CHAPTER 3

Little-Q browsed among the weeds in the fallow land between the horse farm and the cross-cut ditch. He heard the call "kurr-kurr-kurr!" but he did not run to join his friends for a new game. He was out of the mood now.

As he nipped and scratched, he guessed that there was something going on that his folks and the others talked about, but did not want the children to know.

"They always do that," he thought. "It's sort of a game with them." He shrugged and pecked at a grasshopper. "They don't play our games, so I guess we can't play theirs."

His browsing brought him near the ditch, where he heard someone talking. He didn't know anyone was nearby. Yes, there was someone—no, two someones—and they were talking more loudly than he would expect this close to the danger of the road. They were arguing, angrily.

Little-Q cocked his head. "Sounds like old Grackle! The other—" He went over to see what it was all about.

There, on the bank of the narrow, dry ditch, Grackle was pacing up and down and, as usual, talking loudly and making outrageous noises. At the bottom of the ditch, Little-Q saw someone of his people, but not of his covey. Gesturing defiantly and angrily at Grackle was the most beautiful creature he had ever seen. She looked royal.

37

This royal-looking person saw Little-Q peering over the side of the ditch and called out: "Will you please tell this horrible noisy bird to mind his own business!"

Grackle looked at her with a wag of his head, and let out a loud, "Grack!"

Little-Q laughed. "It's only Grackle. He's not angry—unless you're getting in the way of his lunch. He's always noisy and likes to talk a lot."

She wasn't convinced. "He's terrible! Aren't you going to help me?"

The next "Grack!" from Grackle had a sharp tone of frustrated annoyance. "Only! Only—Grackle!"

Little-Q dropped into the ditch. "He sputters and gracks, but I don't think he means to give you a hard time."

"How he frightened me!" she said. "I was making my way down here when all of a sudden this big shape crashes down right next to me and begins making these awful loud noises. Throwing his sharp beak around! Then he goes up there and won't let me out!"

Grackle paused in his pacing and said, "I'm sorry I frightened her. That was not the point I wanted to make. And I am not out to lunch!"

When he paced, his long back feathers swept behind him, making him appear larger and more dignified. He moved deliberately up and down, pecking from time to time at the hard ground.

"It's all right now," Little-Q said. "Why don't you come home with me and have some lunch. You'll like it—we're having a festival."

"Help me get away from him."

"We'll probably have a new game pretty soon and you're welcome to join in."

"Games! I have important business."

"Wait!" Grackle commanded loudly. He stopped pacing and wagged his sharp beak. "You haven't heard what I have to say!"

"I don't think he wants us to leave yet," Little-Q said.

The bird made and awful "Grack!" and pointed his beak at Little-Q and the newcomer at the bottom of the ditch.

"Listen to that!" he shouted.

Little-Q could hear and feel a heavy rumbling vibration, but it seemed no more than what he was used to this close to the road.

"That is the sound of Danger!" Hearing himself make this pronouncement increased Grackle's sense of outrage. His body shook with emotion.

"You!" Grackle pointed at Little-Q threateningly. "You have games! Look, young man—" He paced, shouting and gracking. "You see the world–as—" He stopped, having diffi-culty expressing himself. "To put it in terms which I hope you can understand, let me try to explain this to you. You who live at ground level, so to speak. Do you understand?"

Little-Q was not sure he understood.

Grackle went on: "You have seen me up there at the top of the highest tree? I have a treetop view of life, so I can see every thing. Things you cannot possibly see. Understand?"

Little-Q nodded. Yes, he understood that.

"I have been all over. Listen to me! I tell you that this place is in life-threatening danger!"

Little-Q hoped Grackle would stop soon, so he could get back to the stables and shade.

He wanted to get better acquainted with this beautiful person. It was nice she had dropped in for the festival. Maybe after lunch she would join their games after all.

"First of all," Grackle was saying, "what do you think I am doing here? I'll tell you. I am here with my family because we were pushed out. We are here in this awful desert—you have no idea how green and wonderful life can be—-" He paused and savored the idea. "Yes, green. Soft ground. Juicy bugs."

"If you'll excuse us..." Little-Q began.

Grackle looked at him sharply. "We were pushed out of our home! We ended up here. Look!"

He tilted his head, so that one glinting eye was staring at the ground. He raised up and turned his head to point his beak at the spot on the ground which he eyed so carefully. He struck at the hard dirt, A little dust rose up, but his sharp beak could not penetrate the dry ground,

"That hurts!" he shouted. "Look! Nothing!"

He wiped the dust off his beak.

"I have to fly miles for a meal. Now —" He turned as he was reminded of' what he started to say. "That is the point, You cannot see it from where you are, but I fly around, up high, to the very tree-tops, and I see it. Every day,"

"I'm sure you do," the girl said impatiently, "but if this young man will help me —I have important business —"

Grackle turned full on her, a flash of recognition lighting his eyes. "You there! Now I know you. You are from the north. Am I not correct?"

"That is true. Now I must go—please!"

"Since you are from the north," Grackle said, "you know precisely what is happening to the land. You tell him!"

"Yes! Of course! I know!" She was exasperated with Grackle. "That is why I must leave you. I have important news which I must deliver immediately."

Little-Q saw that she was close to tears. She started to get out of' the ditch. He stepped forward to help, but she waved him regally away.

Grackle stopped her.

"First, tell him!" Grackle raised up on tiptoe in irritated insistence. "Tell him! Tell him —they are coming!"

"They?" Little-Q asked, backing up.

"Yes! They!" Grackle began pacing again.

"What do you mean?" Little-Q asked innocently.

Grackle stopped and shouted at the girl, "You tell him!"

"My message is not for him," she said. "He is a child, only interested in children's games."

Little-Q was suddenly sorry he had invited her to play games. Maybe she would come to the festival anyway.

Grackle was shouting again: "You are in imminent danger — Grack! —You are doomed!"

He took three steps and lifted himself into the air, calling out, "Doomed! Grack! Doomed!"

Grackle circled and flew to the highest tree, pushed a mockingbird off the tallest branch, and took it for himself, still grumbling and grackling at the world.

"I've never seen Grackle so upset," Little-Q said.

The girl lifted herself easily out of the ditch. Little-Q reached to help, but she brushed him off.

"He's gone," the girl said. "Thank you for coming to help me."

"Now we can go to the festival—"

"No! I must see Qwa-say-qua."

"Huh?" Little-Q asked.

"Can you take me to him?"

"Who?"

"The old one who speaks to the Sun. Surely, you know him?"

"Oh!" Little-Q finally understood. "You mean Grandpa!"

"Qwa-say-qua?"

"Yes, he's my grandfather." Little-Q wondered how could a stranger, this beautiful girl from the north, know Grandpa? Know his name!

"Take me to him."

Little-Q led the way, across the fallow land to the path which led to the corral and stables. There was no small talk, and Little-Q felt she held herself aloof, looking down her

41

beak at 'this child.' After a time, he got up nerve to ask her right out how she knew his grandpa.

"I met him some time ago, when he visited my father," she said. "He's very well known for his wisdom and his work with the Old Man of the Mountain and Mr. Sun. He continues to serve, even now, doesn't he?"

Little-Q answered her question over his shoulder as they trotted along, "Sure," as if he knew that. Actually, he was so used to everyone coming to Grandpa with questions that he took it for granted. He began to trot more quickly, and soon they had no breath for talk.

Little-Q was not aware of Grandpa's title, but he knew that Grandpa was one of the elders. It seemed to him that all of the older men were called elders.

He also had noticed that when the men came around to talk to Grandpa, everyone looked very serious. Later, his mother and father would speak together quietly, so that he would not hear. Sometimes they talked for a long time and Little-Q worried that he might have done something wrong that day and they were talking about him.

Little-Q and the girl came out of the field. He led her under the corral fence and they approached the shady place where the men were. Grandpa saw them, stood up and came into the sun to greet the girl.

"Is it Quinata!" he called out. "It's been so long and you've grown up so! What an honor for our covey!"

He turned to the others. "It is Quinata, daughter of Quowson, visiting us from the north. Come, let's welcome her."

The men came up and Quinata bowed. Her movement, while gracious and regal, was not a leisurely luxury; it had a quickness that spoke of her urgency.

"Welcome to our covey!" Papa-Q said. "What a surprise –to have you come for our festival."

Quanute followed and urged her to "Come, eat with us. A splendid feast!"

Uncle-Q added, "Yes, and then you can join our children in the games."

She shook her head. "You are all very kind, but I cannot. I do not have time."

"Come," Grandpa said. "Come into the shade. Gather yourself. You must be exhausted from your travel, you've come so far."

"How did you know it was time for our festival?" Papa asked. "We didn't know ourselves until today."

She did not answer.

Grandpa stood back and studied her.

"You are not here for the festival, are you?" he asked quietly.

"No," she said softly, holding herself in. "Or for the games—" She sobbed.

"Something has happened," Grandpa said.

She nodded silently, barely able to control her distress.

"Tell us. Has something happened to your people—to you?"

"Yes," she said, taking a deep breath. "Many things have happened. The latest right here, but this **young man** came to help I me. I thank him for that."

Little-Q felt himself begin to puff **up, but** immediately was deflated:

"That's just Little-Q," Uncle said. "**He's one** of our little ones.

Quinata turned to find a place to sit, and as she did so, she suddenly lost her self-control and collapsed with a sob, tears filling her eyes. "It's been terrible!"

The men were shocked into full attention.

"What's this?" Papa asked.

Without thinking, Little-Q spoke up, "It was Grackle. He—"

"Hush now," Grandpa ordered. "Let's hear what she has to say."

He indicated to Quinata with a nod of his head that dipped his topknot. "Now, Quinata..."

She swallowed hard, then said with a rush, as if any pause would be filled with a sob: "It's been terrible—awful yellow crawling monsters —a whirlwind of dust devils—so many people lost."

Grandpa leaned forward and touched her lightly, comfortingly. "What has happened? Tell us everything, please."

The men crowded around, and Little-Q stayed as close as he could without getting in the way and having himself shooed off.

Speaking quietly, hesitating now and then to stifle a sob, Quinata began:

"My father and mother and many others have been hurt. I was one of the lucky ones. I escaped and came to ask you —."

"Of course!" Old Quaymon broke in. "We will come fight—"

"Wait!" Grandpa commanded. He nodded to Quinata.

She went on: "The big machines came at first light, without warning. Yes, there was something. A little one, the color of the poison butterfly, had come onto our land before."

"All that one did was raise much dust, and after it left, life went back to normal. There was some wondering, what was it all about, but we weren't really worried."

"Then, suddenly, today, very early—" she glanced at Grandpa.

Grandpa nodded encouragingly. "Yes?"

She lowered her head and sobbed. "Instead of brightness, this day brought..."

Old Quaymon jumped up excitedly: "Let's go get them! Now!"

"Wait!" Grandpa commanded. "Control yourself. Give her a chance —"

"They were insatiable monsters!" Quinata said. "Sweeping over the land! Tearing up the ground! Making the dust rise like a storm! Eating everything in the way. Our homes, our food. Everything!"

She stopped a few moments, breathing quickly. "Everything—just gone."

Old Quaymon shouted: "I've heard enough! Let's go battle these awful things!"

Quinata looked at him with such an expression—her sad hurt contrasting with his impulsive anger—that he stepped back, almost embarrassed.

In a rush of words, she went on: "It was like a caterpillar stripping a leaf. So big! So noisy! So quick! Some of the men tried to protect us any way they could. They were the first to go. Those of us who could still move after the first sweep ran to the ditches. Then some of the ditches were covered over. One place, the one my father and mother and I managed to reach, was somehow left alone."

She gasped for breath. "Father was hurt and Mother, too. He would never ask for help, and he doesn't know that I'm here."

She took a deep breath and went on:

"It's all so awful. So many hurt. So many lost. Our homes gone —"

At the words, she broke down. The men looked at each other, shaking their heads angrily. The mood had changed from a festival gladness to deadly life-and-death seriousness as they came to realize that this had happened over the horizon in the land to the north.

"This is terrible!" Grandpa said. "You must join us here. We will send our best men to guide your people."

The men stood silently before her quiet sobbing. Grandpa and Papa-Q exchanged glances. They stepped away from the others and spoke softly.

"If it has happened there, " Papa-Q said, "could it happen here?"

"I was thinking the same thing," Grandpa said.

They went back to the group.

"Can you tell us a little more about the warning sign which you had before the coming of this devastation?"

Old Quaymon broke in: "Yes! What should we look for?"

"Yes," Quyor said, "our families..."

She shook her head, disturbed by the memory. "A little time before, there was a smaller one, like one of the monster's babies. Even that did not seem so much out of place at the time. Sometimes these things come onto your land, and then after a time, they go away. It was the color of the poison butterfly."

"If we knew the signs," Quanute objected, "and wanted to move our families, where would we go?"

"Yes!" Quyor said suddenly, as the idea struck home. "Where could we go in this day and age?"

"I think it's just an isolated incident," someone said.

"I'm not so sure we're in danger here."

Little-Q spoke up with his news: "Grackle says we are all doomed. We saw him, didn't we?" He looked to Quinata for support—" and he said we are in awful danger, and—"

He stopped when he noticed the look Papa-Q shot his way.

"This is pretty serious," Papa said, "We must get Quinatas people down here where they will be safe."

"Perhaps," Grandpa said thoughtfully, "we should send someone to scout out possibilities for our move. Just in case."

"Yes," Quanute said. "Perhaps go back to the wash or find some other place we could move to, if—-"

"My family is not going to the wash," Uncle-Q said.

"Not so fast!" someone objected. "I don't think we need to move. There's no need to panic."

Others took up the point: "Our place is peaceful."

"Look around at how quiet it is. Even the horses are gone."

"We'll be fine."

Old Quaymon shouted: "You fools! You complacent fools! Don't you see — !"

As Old Quaymon was shouting, one of the other elders leaned close to Papa-Q and whispered softly. An occasional phrase could be heard by the others— "Just a girl...wild story... can't happen here... ideal without the horses shouldn't panic over this..."

Papa pulled away and shook his head, and said loudly, for all to hear: "Grandpa is right. We must take precautions."

"Yes, but—"the other objected.

Grandpa made a sign to break in, and turned back to Quinata. "First of all, Quinata, we would welcome your people to come here and make a new home with us."

"Thank you," she said.

"Where are your father and mother? Are they able to travel?"

"I left them in a protected place. I hope there are others."

"We must send men to help deal with this attack on the land to the north," Grandpa said, looking around at the men. "Who would be best—"

Old Quaymon was on his tiptoes, waving: "Let me!"

Grandpa turned to speak, but he was interrupted by the noise of a machine entering the land.

Small, yellow, moving quickly, the machine swerved toward the stable area. It ran directly between the watering trough and the buildings. It kicked up a cloud of dust, throwing off chunks of dirt and gravel. The people ran for the shelter of the stable.

47

"That's it!" Quinata cried. "That's the one! That's the baby monster that came on our land!"

Cringing backward toward the fence, the elders and Quinata watched in horror as the machine moved quickly across the corral, turned with a dust-raising skid, and headed back.

All but Grandpa. After a moment of surprise, he recovered himself and stepped forward, facing the danger. Papa-Q joined him, and Old Quaymon ran to stand with them. They stood tall with topknots up high, between the others and the machine.

Papa-Q turned to Grandpa. "It is the color of the poison butterfly."

Grandpa nodded with a determined expression. At that moment, Little-Q glimpsed in his kindly old grandfather the qualities of the ancient warriors of the Q-clan.

CHAPTER 4

The machine stopped abruptly. During the moment or two it seemed to catch its breath, women and children ran for the nesting ground. The elders—Quinata and Little-Q with them—were cut off and could only watch as the machine started up again.

It began to browse around the land, more slowly now, but with turns so abrupt that it raised new clouds of dust.

The machine nosed into corner, twisted back, and set off again, stopping now and then to plant a peculiar flat flower with a short skinny stalk. It was the color of the poison butterfly.

"That's just what it did on our land," Quinata said.

"They must be poison!" Papa-Q said.

After a time, the machine stopped, breathing hard, apparently satiated. All at once, it made a loud noise and sped out of the land, raising more dust to mark its trail.

"It has poisoned our land," Papa said angrily.

"We cannot stay here," Grandpa-Q said with sad determination. "We must get organized for action. I want to talk to the messengers and scouts."

Grandpa instructed Little-Q to take Quinata to Mama-Q. "Hurry! Before it comes back!"

Little-Q groaned with disappointment. He did not want to miss any of the excitement, and going off with this girl meant he was sure to lose out on something.

Papa's sharp look and "Quickly, Little-Q!" command overcame his hesitation.

Little-Q hurried with Quinata down the path beside the line of fence posts toward the nesting grounds. Part way, she stopped him.

"Where are the horses?" she asked. "I always heard that a family of horses lived with you and they shared your food and water, and that even on the coldest day they were never without. Yet today—-"

"They have left us," Little-Q interrupted. "It's okay. We have more room to play now. It's too bad you missed our festival games. "

"Games! Children's games! How can you play children's games after everything that's happened!"

Little-Q realized that he had said the wrong thing, but he meant to be nice. He hoped she would not start crying again.

He stopped and turned to her. "I'm sorry," he said. "It was a dumb thing to say, but I wanted to cheer you up."

They went on more slowly. He did wish he could stop saying dumb things and stop acting like a little kid.

"I never heard of horses migrating," she said. "Why would they leave you at this time of year..."

When they reached the nesting ground, he led Quinata through the growth at the edge of the path. In a sheltered place under the low-hanging branches of an old palo verde tree, Mama-Q was talking with Grandma and Aunt-Q.

Aunt saw him first.

"Is it gone?" she exclaimed, going on without a breath. "Are you all right? What a scare! This is all too much for me. I need to get home. No matter what, I want to get across the water and home. Who is that with you?"

Quinata stepped forward, and Little-Q introduced her.

"This is Quinata from the north. They've had a lot of trouble and her mother and father have been hurt and she came to us and Grandpa says—"

"Welcome, Quinata," Mama-Q interrupted. "Come into the shade and cool yourself and rest."

Grandma-Q spoke up: "Now that I can see her, she looks awful, poor child! What has happened to you?"

The women swept her into their care, and Mama-Q said, "You'll be all right with us. Little-Q, you run along."

That was fine with him because now he could run back to the corral and stables and not be left out of the excitement. On the trail, he passed Old Quaymon. Both were in such a hurry, they rushed past each other with hardly a nod.

A messenger also ran past him, running in the direction of the corral. It seemed everyone was running every which way. It was exciting to see so much going on, even though it was scary to have that strange thing come onto the land.

The corral area was bustling with activity and chatter.

At the big stump, Grandpa-Q gathered the messengers to report what they knew of the day's events. The elders were there to hear.

"I think that the more we know, the better," Grandpa told Papa-Q. "Quickly, quickly. I feel an urgency about this whole situation."

"As far as we know, no one was hurt," Papa-Q said. "It was a good scare."

"Perhaps more than a scare," Grandpa said.

One of the young messengers excitedly began to tell the elders about the yellow machine.

"Yes, thank you," Grandpa said, stopping him as he prepared to act out the swerves and skids.

Another said his father had seen Hawk circling in the north sky. That was disturbing, because it usually meant

51

something bad had happened on the ground, or would soon if Hawk saw a target to dive on.

A third messenger reported that his grandmother had seen three starlings on a fence. "She says that is a sign—a sign of trouble. Bad trouble."

Little-Q told about his encounter with Grackle and how he had saved the beautiful Quinata from the north.

"Saved her!" one of his friends laughed. "Saved her from that old loud-mouth! He's just a lot of talk."

"Yeah!" another put in. "It was probably Grackle that saved her from you!"

Quyor broke in: "Quiet down, boys! This is serious business. No time for that!"

"Yes, we are facing a serious crisis here," elder Quanute started in a speechy sort of way. "It may affect the whole future of the covey and even of our people."

Grandpa-Q gestured and quieted the diversion.

"Settle down, lads, and pay attention, very carefully," he said. "We do have some serious business here. You have a vital message to take back to the families."

Someone interrupted to ask about Quinata.

"Old Quaymon is taking her back to her land," he said. "They should be on their way now."

So that's where Old Quaymon was going! Little-Q realized. Quinata was going back to the north already! With a touch of regret, it occurred to him that he might not see her again. He wanted to make things right between them—show her that he was interested in more than games.

Grandpa-Q came back to the warning Little-Q had heard from Grackle. "That can be serious, although Grackle's talk is difficult to make sense of at times."

"It makes more sense now that we've heard what happened in the north," Papa said.

"What does it all mean?" one of the elders asked. "What message do you want them to take back to the families?"

Grandpa turned to the young messengers: "Tell your people to be prepared to move. We don't know, at this time, when that might be or where we might go. That's all we can say for now."

"Move!" someone exclaimed. "We don't do that anymore. We're not like the others."

"My mom," another voice piped up, "has said a thousand times that she never wants to go back to the Wash."

Elder Quanute said: "That's one of the issues the elders will have to evaluate. If we move, and when, and where."

The others looked to Grandpa to see if that was really the answer. He nodded. "Quanute has expressed it perfectly," Grandpa said. "The episode we had today may be an isolated incident, or it may be the first sign of worse things to come. You youngsters get along. Send out the word."

As the messengers moved off, Grandpa and the elders put their heads together, beaks almost touching. It looked very serious to Little-Q. He could hear them beginning to argue one side and then the other.

"What do you make of it all?" Quyor asked. "Could it really be as bad up north as the girl says? Do you think such a thing could happen to us here?"

"That machine was nothing special," someone else put in. "We've seen things like that before.

"Not that color," another objected, "or acting so crazy."

"Yes, but—" another said, "what we have to live with here is so good it would be foolish to leave it for no good reason."

"How can you think of staying after what it did to our land! You can see its tracks right there—and there—!"

"Yes, it poisoned the land."

"We're not sure of that."

Grandpa-Q listened intently as the talk went back and forth.

53

"If we have to move," Quyor said, "where would we go?" I heard someone say, 'Back to the Wash,' but that was a bad time for our people."

"My grandparents came here from the Wash," Uncle-Q said. "I've decided to stay where we are."

"You always did prefer that, didn't you?" Papa-Q said. "I could never understand how you could stand the noise at your place—that awful singing and the water!"

"You get used to it, and talk louder." Uncle-Q laughed. "It's getting a little overgrown, but that's all right." He lowered his voice and added, "Frankly, those horses were too much for me." Then, to all, "No Wash for my family, thank you!"

"I vote with Uncle-Q," Quyor announced. "I don't want to move my family to the Wash. Not after what happened to my grand-dad."

"How much do we know about the Wash?" Papa asked. "Or what there is in the land beyond?"

A surprised shout interrupted the debate:

"Look! See there!"

Across the corral, a sparrow pecked at one of the flat yellow flowers left by the machine.

"We must stop him!"

"Too late! He's got it!"

The sparrow opened its beak and bit the strange blossom.

"Nothing happened!"

The sparrow dropped it and flew away.

"See there! It must not be poison."

"Yes, but—the color..."

"If they're not poison, we could stay here, couldn't we?"

Grandpa shook his head with disapproval. "I wouldn't want one of our people trying that."

At that moment, one of the covey children ran out and pecked one of the flat yellow flowers. He took the bit of yellow in its beak and shook it like a bug.

A father began to run, shouting: "Stop! Stop!"

The little one dropped the thing and went for a snack at another place nearby.

The elders, who watched in silent horror, laughed with relief to see the little one walk away unharmed. In a minute or two, other Covey children were pecking and pulling at the peculiar yellow flowers.

Soon the whole crop was pulled up and scattered.

"That's the end of that!" Uncle-Q said.

"I must say," Grandpa laughed, "that's a frightening way to learn that lesson."

"Now!" one of the elders said triumphantly, "that really opens up our discussion."

"Yes," Grandpa agreed. "Even with that demonstration, I believe the safety of' the covey is our first responsibility."

Little-Q felt a punch in his side. It was Cousin-Q. "This is boring," he said. "Let's go someplace."

Little-Q nodded. "All they do is talk and not really decide anything. "

As they left the elders, Little-Q asked his cousin what he thought.

"I guess something is going on," Cousin said. "Maybe your folks will go someplace, but I'm glad we get to stay across the water. It's kind of closed in, but my dad says that's what makes it good."

They were interrupted by a messenger back from his errand, who called out, "Hey, watch this!" He was running and swerving and kicking up dust, imitating the yellow machine that had been on the land.

"Me too!" another called. "Look at me! I'm the baby monster! Can't catch me!"

"Come on, Little-Q!" Cousin said. "Let's play baby monster!"

Little-Q did not feel like playing games.

He was not comfortable with all this playing around at a time when his father and the other men were so serious. Something must be in the air. Then there was that girl from the north who seemed so different, and what had happened to her family.

He looked back and saw the dust which was kicked up by the children playing baby monster. Overhead, he saw Hawk, high up, wings wide, circling slowly, lazing in wide circles, above the land to the north.

He came to realize that the episode with the machine was not something for a game.

"I wonder what will happen now," he thought.

He must have said it out loud, because he heard an answer which startled him. He saw Sparrow, dusting himself on the ground nearby.

"What did you say?" Little-Q asked.

"I said not to worry," Sparrow said, fluffing the dust through his feathers.

"I didn't mean to disturb you. I didn't see you here." "Yes, you seemed quite lost in thought. You know, I was having second breakfast at the stable when the machine raised all that dust. I say, don't worry about it."

"Grackle says we are doomed. That was the exact word he said. Doomed! I think that's scary."

"What does he know? Such a noisy loudmouth. Don't tell him I said so. He has such a sharp beak."

"He flies all over and sees everything and—"

"We get around a bit, too, you know. We've seen things like this a hundred times and, look, we're not bothered. We fly with it, and after the dust settles we move in with them."

"Move in with them?"

"Whatever comes up after all the machines get done. You see, more machines come after, and they plant things, and pretty soon you have something brand-new right there. That's fine because there's more to eat than ever before. I don't think you have a thing to worry about. Just be above it all."

Little-Q thought about this and said, "That makes me feel a little better. I'm still not sure that what works for you people will work for us."

He saw Papa-Q come away from the meeting. "There's my dad. I've got to go."

Papa-Q was going toward the nesting place. Little-Q ran to catch up.

"Hi, there!" Papa said when Little-Q caught up. "Glad you're here! Come with me —we've got some important things to do."

Little-Q trotted grandly beside his father. Papa-Q clapped him on the shoulder. "I have a special job for you. Very special."

They hurried down the path, Little-Q running to keep up. Then turned to go through the grass, which grew along the fence line and into the opening that led to the cover of the old palo verde.

The women gave them an anxious welcome.

"We didn't expect you so soon," Mama-Q said. "Where's Grandpa?"

"Still at the meeting. He wanted us to get started right away."

She looked questioningly from one to the other. Little-Q had no idea what his Papa had in mind, but enjoyed being part of the activity.

"What's going on?" Mama-Q asked. "Are we going to have to move or will we stay here?"

Aunt-Q spoke up: "I do hope that everyone can keep the home they have. It's been so handy to visit back and forth, and you have so many nice things on this side of the water."

Papa-Q did not have time for small talk. "Did Old Quaymon and the girl get off all right?"

"Yes, fine," Grandma-Q said. "She's in such a state, but she's so brave. It's just horrible when those yellow monsters come on the land and tear up your whole life in just minutes. Everything gone!"

"Tell us what the elders have decided," Mama-Q said.

"We're guessing that the little one we saw this morning was, a scout and there's a possibility that was the end of it. On the other hand—"

"Yes?"

"You never know. We have to be prepared for anything that might happen."

Little-Q spoke up excitedly. "Grackle says—"

His father interrupted him sharply. "We sent Old Quaymon with Quinata back to her land to see what can be done. They will return with her family—her people—as quickly as they can. As many as are able to travel. We'll care for them here."

"And our people..." Mama-Q asked.

"Since we appear to be in no immediate danger, we will plan to stay here, for now. We have plenty, of course, even for when the cold comes back. Meantime..."

When he stopped, Mama asked, "Meantime?"

"One of the elders will scout out possibilities for a new home for the Covey," Papa said, adding quickly, "Just in case, you understand."

"Yes, of course. Just in case."

"Not the Wash, surely," Grandma said.

"There's talk of a land beyond the Wash," Papa said.

Everyone was silent a moment. It was difficult to take it all in, so quickly. Each had questions, but each held their doubts and fears and worries to themselves for a few moments.

Little-Q felt that there was more going on than he was aware of. He held his breath, not wanting to break the quiet. "Be grown up," he told himself. "This is real. This is serious."

After a time, Mama-Q spoke softly. "And who is the brave elder who will go out to scout the land for our future home?"

Mention of a future home was followed by a ripple of comments about moving or not moving. Papa waited for the voices to subside into quiet.

"I am to go," he said, making an effort to appear casual. He went on, almost jokingly, "I'll go out and do some scouting around. See some new country. It won't take a day or two. It will be fun for me, and you folks will do just fine while I'm gone. Little-Q will be here, and Grandpa and Uncle-Q. You'll do fine."

"Of course, you must go," Mama said. "You're the finest scout in the covey, and you will do the best."

"If you go," Grandma said, "then who—?"

Papa shook his head warningly, and looked sideways in the direction of Little-Q. He wanted to speak to his son first about what had been decided, before discussing the matter in public.

Grandma insisted. "Who is going to help Grandpa at the Tall Pole?"

Papa looked at Little-Q with a nod and everyone understood. Little-Q drew back slightly, surprised and a bit overwhelmed.

"Why not your brother, Uncle-Q?" Mama-Q asked.

"He couldn't do anything like that," Aunt-Q said. "He's got to get his family back home. Besides, I don't want him crossing the water during the time of the darkness."

"Little-Q?" Grandma said doubtfully. "What will Grandpa say?"

"It was Grandpa's idea."

Little-Q was not sure he wanted the honor of going to the Tall Pole with Grandpa-Q. To work with Grandpa! At the Tall Pole! He did not know what to do or what was expected of him. He remembered hearing his father get up in the dark,

59

and how comfortable it felt to go back to sleep after Papa had gone out to meet Grandpa and go with him in the darkness to the Tall Pole.

CHAPTER 5

Later, Papa asked Little-Q to walk with him down the path he was taking to begin his scouting mission into the unknown land. The Tall Pole was far behind them, facing the Old Man of the Mountain.

"All set for tomorrow, Little-Q?" Papa asked.

"Sure," Little-Q said, a little unsurely.

"Doesn't sound like it to me."

"I don't know what I'm supposed to do. Besides, I'm not—I don't feel..."

His words came out whiny, and Little-Q did not like to sound that way. He wasn't whining. He really was not sure how he would do at the Tall Pole with Grandpa. Besides, you did need to have your name before you could do anything important in the covey.

"It will be all right," Papa said. "This is a special time. An emergency, sort of. Grandpa will teach you what you need to know. He'll show you what to do."

"I'm not even sure I can wake up in time."

"Don't worry. He'll come for you. You'll do fine."

"I hope so."

Papa stopped and touched Little-Q's shoulder.

"Look, Little-Q, this is very important. To me, to your mother, to the whole covey. I have to go out there," he pointed. "So you will have to be the man of the family for a while. You will have to be the adult now."

"I do want to. But I'm not sure I'll do right."

"Your mother says you have the stuff of heroes in you, and I'm inclined to agree with her. I'm sure you'll do a great job."

"I'll try. I promise. No more kid stuff."

Little-Q gazed at the horizon, which overlooked the end of the world, and asked, "How will you know where to go?"

Papa pointed. "Do you see the Day-Star way out there? Grandpa showed me how to guide on it. In fact, his grandfather made it their Tall Pole when the covey's home was near the end of the world. They were flooded out and he had to move his work to a new Tall Pole—the one we have now."

He went on with his explanation as they resumed walking, more slowly now. "The Day-Star is as far as anyone has gone. If I go beyond that—"

The path, seldom traveled to this distance, was becoming scraggly and overgrown. Papa stopped. "I go alone from here. You go back. Remember what I told you."

"You mean, you're going now?" Little-Q was beginning to realize what was expected of him. "I go with Grandpa tomorrow?"

Papa laughed. "Yes, of course! You are now the man of our family."

Papa left quickly. After a few steps, he stopped, turned and waved.

"Good-bye! Remember—!" He swung back to face the Day Star.

Little-Q watched Papa-Q trot down the path. He was soon at the turn and, suddenly, he was out of sight. Just beyond the curve, Little-Q knew, the path disappeared. He'd been taught never to go out there.

Little-Q felt himself sob inside. "Papa?" he whispered. It was all happening so fast!

Little-Q took a deep breath and straightened himself. He walked slowly back toward the nesting ground.

That evening, Mama-Q reminded Little-Q that he must go to sleep early. "You have a big day tomorrow." He was wide-awake and full of doubt about his new work.

She frizzled her beak softly through his back feathers.

"There must be a dozen in the covey who would give their topknot to go out with your grandpa to the Tall Pole. You seem not so sure. What is it?"

After a hesitation, his frustrations poured out, just as they had when he talked with Papa-Q.

"I'm not sure I can do it right. I don't know what I'm supposed to do. I'm still a kid."

She understood. "Are you worried that you will go to the Tall Pole with Grandpa without—?" She didn't complete the sentence, but Little-Q knew what she meant. "Is that it?"

"Yes, I guess so. It's just that everything is happening so fast."

She tried to reassure him. "There's so much confusion in our lives now. There hasn't been time. I'm sure when things settle down. Unless—"

"Unless? "

"I have heard stories, when it just happened to someone in very special circumstances."

She sat up and lifted his face with her wing so that she was looking into his eyes. "Grandpa selected you, out of all the others. I know you're the right one."

Little-Q still wasn't sure. Was what he said the real reason, or was it the idea of being awakened to go out into the dark?

"When you go out there with Grandpa tomorrow," Mama went on, "you'll be so busy you'll forget all your worries."

"Maybe."

She took him in her wing. Her voice changed from soothing mother-comforter to a level of seriousness.

"Listen, Little-Q, carefully," she said. "I know you have the stuff of heroes in you. I knew you in your egg. You are going to do great things for your people and this is just the start."

"In my egg?"

"I felt you moving one morning, and I sang to you and spoke to you and told you stories of Hero-Q, and we were friends even before you were strong enough to come out."

He had never heard this.

"You were very special because you were the only one left after that awful night when Jackrabbit and Dog came crashing through and scattered my nest and broke up everything. How awful that was!" She shuddered at the remembrance of it. "Papa found you. You were the only one. We worked through the dark to make a new nest for you and— here you are!"

So! That was why he had no brothers or sisters.

"Even more important," Mama-Q said softly, "when you finally came out of your egg, you had the sweetest, bravest smile. You looked right past me. I looked where you were looking. There in the sky was a beautiful feather, our most powerful sign for a newborn. That's when I chose my name for you."

"That doesn't come until—" he said.

"Yes, I know. We'll see if the one you are given is anything like the one I have for you. If my feeling is right, and I'm sure it is because I have a mother's feeling about it, it will be the very same."

"What is it?"

"I can't tell you. Just as you must never talk about it. Its meaning is that you will be brave and full of courage. Like Hero-Q himself."

"How will I learn these things? Will Papa come back and teach me? Or Grandpa? Or the old men?"

"You already know," she said. "It's like flying. You already know. You just have to do it. To try. Then you will know that you know."

Little-Q felt he had hardly been asleep when Mama-Q was nudging him awake. He tried to become alert as he remembered what he was to do, but his head was too full of sleep. Grandpa was there. Respecting the deepness of the hour, no one spoke aloud. Mama-Q whispered, "Are you all right?"

Little-Q nodded.

"Are you really?" she asked.

He nodded again, shaking and stretching to bring awakeness through his feathers.

Grandpa said in a very soft voice, "We must go."

Little-Q nodded. His mother nudged him, and he followed as Grandpa stepped out.

The darkness was so strong on the ground that Little-Q could not see where he was walking. He looked up. In the sky were many tiny points of brightness.

This was the ground where he played every day, but he recognized none of it in the blackness which seemed to go behind his eyes. How would they find the Tall Pole? he wondered.

It was all so strange, and a little frightening. He had seen the darkness from a distance, once or twice when he went on playing after his mother called. This was so different! He stayed close to Grandpa.

At the top of the rise, Grandpa stopped. He was alert and fresh, full of life.

"Look," he said enthusiastically, pointing at the sky.

"You'll learn about the hero stars one day, and—look there!" He pointed: "That very bright one, above the edge of the world, we will guide on that." He started off again. "Quickly, now. Quickly."

Little-Q tried to take it all in and was still staring at the sky when Grandpa stopped and called back to him. "Come! Quickly!"

Little-Q ran to catch up. He could make out the faint outline of the Old Man of the Mountain against the far horizon.

Beyond, a dim lightness quavered, as if a struggle was going on behind the Old Man of the Mountain.

Grandpa stopped to feel around in the growth off to the side. He brought out a stick. He handed it to Little-Q. It felt smooth and worn along the body. One end narrowed to a point.

"Here, quickly," Grandpa said, urging Little-Q forward. "You see?"

Little-Q had been here with Papa-Q to mark the festival time, but now nothing was familiar. Somehow, the darkness, Grandpa's urgency, his serious manner, changed all that was common to him in the bright day into something mysterious.

Before them was a stark shadow-shape rising against the sky. It was the Tall Pole, standing alone at the highest point at the farthest reach of the covey land.

Grandpa hurried to the pole, Little-Q with him.

"Stop here," Grandpa said. At their feet was the broad flat stone which circled the pole.

"This is important," Grandpa said. "Here is what you are to do. At the very moment Mr. Sun breaks his light on the pole, he will make his shadow appear. You stand here. You must mark that point exactly."

He showed Little-Q a place at the edge of the stone.

"No matter what happens, you must stay and make your mark,"

Grandpa said. "The exact moment! Understand?"

"Yes! I'll do it!"

Grandpa trotted quickly beyond the pole, toward the edge of the world.

Little-Q felt a rise of energy in his chest, realizing that he had not said, "I'll try," but " I will do it!"

He called out loudly, "I will do it, Grandpa! I will do it." Grandpa was out of sight in the dark.

Little-Q gripped the stick and stared at the dark shape of the Tall Pole, ready to act. It seemed to him that he waited a very long time. His grip on the stick eased. He felt a part of himself going back to sleep. His head wavered.

Suddenly, in the sky, a single point of light glinted more brightly than the others. It must be one of the Hero Stars! For an instant only, it flashed brilliantly in his eye. Little-Q shook his head. Had the Hero Star spoken to him, somehow, with that flash? The strange incident brought him awake.

He took a deep breath, stretched tall and waved the stick high. "I will do it!" he said aloud. Then he shouted: "I will make my mark!"

A cry from Grandpa startled him. The cry was urgent, yet went on a little time in a singing sort of way. Little-Q cocked his head. Was Grandpa all right?

Little-Q had the impulse to run and help. The stick in his hand reminded him of what Grandpa told him: "Stay and make your mark."

His whole body focused concentration on the place the sound came from.

All at once, he saw the shadow-shape of Grandpa rise up and step to the very edge of the world.

A dark rumbling responded, as if echoing from conflict far beyond the Old Man of the Mountain.

Grandpa-Q stood tall, topknot outlined against the sky, his wings raised wide. He called out a beautiful song Little-Q had never heard before.

A beginning of light moved in the sky. It slowly dissolved the darkness with a majesty that made Little-Q's feathers move.

He stared in wonder. He felt himself quake with a deep resonance that had been dormant in him before this moment.

Grandpa cried out. At that instant, a sliver of brightness shot through a V in the Old Man of the Mountain. The point of light glinted in his eyes and made him blink.

Little-Q looked down and as quickly as he did so, a dark line—the shadow of Mr. Sun's new light—appeared on the Great Stone before him.

At the place Grandpa had shown him, Little-Q pressed hard with the stick against the stone and made his mark. All at once, all around him, he felt the world come awake.

Just as quickly, Grandpa was at his side.

"Did you get it?" Grandpa was breathing hard, as if he had made a long uphill run.

"Yes, I got it! Right here!"

Grandpa checked his work. "Yes. Yes. Good!" He patted Little-Q on the shoulder approvingly. "Good."

He walked around the Pole, studying the stone and the earth around it. From time to time he nodded and said, "Good. Good. He's coming along. The hot will go. Yes, sooner than we think."

When he circled back to where Little-Q was standing, he took the marking stick and leaned over the stone.

"Now, we must confirm that as a permanent mark on the Great Stone."

As Grandpa concentrated on the markings, Little-Q watched intently. "I was here with Papa, but I never noticed all that."

"No, of course not," Grandpa said. "Many things remain unnoticed, perhaps hidden, until we need them, or until we understand their use."

He raised up and stretched.

"You can learn," Grandpa said. "I know you can, when you are ready. It's too bad our arrangement is temporary. I would like to be the one to teach you, as I taught your father."

Grandpa hefted the marking stick. "I'll show you where we stash this, in case you are needed again some day."

"Papa will be back and come with you tomorrow, won't he?"

"Yes, of course, and the work will go on. It must. So much depends on it. So much."

Grandpa showed him the secret place to cache the marking stick and then, free of the day's obligation, gave Little-Q a friendly tap on the shoulder.

"How about some breakfast?" he said. "I think we've earned it, don't you?"

"I'd like that," Little-Q said, stepping off with Grandpa down the trail.

They went down toward the stables, the sun blazing at their backs.

"It's hot already, isn't it?" Little-Q said.

"It's a little better than yesterday, and tomorrow will be a little more better, I'm sure. It's coming along nicely this year."

CHAPTER 6

Little-Q was so excited by his experience at the Tall Pole that he began to strut around and expected everyone to congratulate him.

Grandpa cautioned him about making a show or bragging about what he did.

"The work itself is reward enough," he said. "If you do it for any other reason, you could lose it."

Little-Q settled down while the covey came together for breakfast. Soon everyone was so busy eating there was little conversation.

The quiet was broken by a shout, "He's back! He's back!"

Little-Q jumped up to run—"Papa's back!"—but stopped when he heard: "It's Old Quaymon! Old Quaymon is back!"

"Good," someone said nearby. "Now we'll learn something."

"Yes, news about what's happening up north. So often what happens to them one season comes to us the next."

"He'll probably have Quinata's people with him."

Old Quaymon did not. He reported to the group of elders who gathered in the shade across from the stable.

"Everything is fine!" he said. "It's not as bad as they first thought. They are going to stay and are busy rebuilding."

He told the elders that Quinata's father was upset because she had left the covey to go for help. Her mother welcomed her and smoothed the old man's ruffled feathers. They were very glad to see her. They were afraid she'd been lost in the attack.

"He said they really didn't need help," Old Quaymon said. "He sent me away."

"But the monsters?" someone asked.

"They stopped in their tracks and haven't moved since the first day."

When the monsters were quiet for a very long time, he explained, the covey people finally went near them, carefully. Nothing happened. After a time, some of the children began to play around them.

"One even lighted right on a monster, and that gave everyone a good scare. Nothing happened. They got braver and braver. Little by little, more and more people—young and old–went on them. Right onto them! They found them altogether lifeless."

Old Quaymon interrupted the murmurs of surprise to say, "So they decided to stay there."

"It's not natural," someone objected, "having big yellow monsters roosting on your land."

"Maybe they're sleeping," another said. "Might spring to life at any moment and—whoosh! There you go!"

Old Quaymon continued: "After they told me all that, they sent me away. Quowson said that he's sorry that his daughter alarmed us, and wishes us well."

"Did you actually see these monsters, Quaymon?" Grandpa-Q asked.

"Yes, I did," Old Quaymon said seriously. "Awfully big. As big as this—" he gestured toward the stable building"—and ugly. Unnaturally shaped. Hard to see how they get around, without wings or legs or anything. They do, and most powerfully, too, they say. Very dangerous to be near, when they are alive and awake and moving every which way."

"Did you go near one?"

Old Quaymon brushed the ground with a tip of a wing and swung his body, somewhat embarrassed.

"I'm no hero, you know, but—" he paused. "Yes, I not only went near, but onto it. Had to fly up, it's so high, as tall as some of our trees, but it's true, all they said."

"What happened then? What was it like?"

"Nothing happened," Old Quaymon answered. "Lifeless. Not asleep, mind you, but no life at all that I could tell."

He paused a moment, reflecting, then went on:

"It must have been an awful sight to see them move and knock things down and throw the earth into the air, but as they are now, just lying there, lifeless, Quinata's people aren't worried."

"That's good news," someone said.

"Yes," Uncle-Q said, "if the monsters are lying lifeless on the land to the north, it's not likely we will ever see them here."

"That's right," another said. "We haven't seen the baby one since he came scouting the land. That's a good sign."

"Perhaps it was just a random raid sort of thing—nothing serious," someone else suggested. "A bit of playing around by some maverick, a kind of game for them."

"Some game!"

"That's a good sign for us. If Quinata's people are not pushed off their land, we won't be bothered either."

"We don't need to move!"

"Yes! We can stay right here."

"Let's vote on it!" a voice exclaimed. The suggestion was followed by a common assent, and Grandpa went around the circle, asking each one: "All right, what say you?"

They said, "Stay," or nodded or grunted their agreement.

When he completed the circle, Grandpa said: "It's settled, then. We'll stay."

Little-Q was hovering at the edge of all the talk, and when he heard the conclusion he quickly asked Grandpa if he could run and tell his mother that they were going to stay on their land.

"When Papa gets back," Little-Q said, "everything will be just like before!"

He ran off before Grandpa could answer. The group began to break up.

Uncle-Q remained to ask Grandpa: "You don't seem to be altogether comfortable with this decision."

"I guess it's all right for now. We must be alert. I'm having second thoughts about sending out Papa-Q to scout new land. In the light of this information, it may not be all that urgent now."

"Don't worry—he'll be back any minute," Uncle-Q said, turning to leave. "Before the dark for sure."

"Yes, of course. Yes."

Old Quaymon stood quietly beside Grandpa. When they were alone, Grandpa turned to face him.

"Good report," Grandpa said. "Thanks for going up there. It's very helpful to have first-hand information. Tell me, old friend, what do you really think of' all this?"

Old Quaymon scratched the dirt a bit and squirmed his shoulders. "There is one thing I didn't mention. They took me to a place north of their land where the yellow monsters were seen some time ago. It was a place of total destruction. The land was swept clean of' everything useful to a covey. Would not support life as we know it. You wouldn't recognize it as good for any thing."

Old Quaymon looked around, leaned close to Grandpa and went on:

"Privately, Quinata's father told me that this was not the first. They heard of others farther away, pecking away at the land little by little."

Grandpa shook his head sadly, and asked, "What does it all mean?"

"He thinks everything north of the water could be at risk. But he wants to stay on their land and see it through."

"It's like the night of falling stars," Grandpa said. "Is there anything that can be done?"

"There was one other thing," Old Quaymon said. "They think the cold stops them. They have heard that when the cold is so bad you can hardly move, these monster stop moving."

"Perhaps they hibernate in some strange way?" Grandpa asked.

"They are strange creatures. If the cold comes soon – What do you think, Grandpa? How soon can we expect the cold?"

"It will be some time yet before the real cold. That may be too far away to do us any good. We'll have to see."

Life in the covey was soon back to normal for everyone except Little-Q. He kept going down to the path to look at the Day Star, hoping to see Papa-Q trotting back. Papa-Q did not return, and Little-Q understood that he would go again to the Tall Pole with Grandpa.

After the last feeding, as the covey gathered in and around the old palo verde, Grandma-Q said, "I'm glad that's over–that scare about moving. I'm really glad it isn't like when our people had to leave the Wash in such a rush, or even the night the stars fell."

"What's that all about, Grandma?" Little-Q asked.

"When the Covey people moved before..." she said. "A story of our history."

"Tell us a story, Grandma!"

"Not tonight. You have to be up early. Besides, it's hard to remember them offhand like this. If we had the Memory Stick..."

"I've never seen the Memory Stick."

"You're too young to know about that, aren't you," she said.

"It's a very special thing, very old, shaped just right. If you know the stick you can rub it here and there and it will sing to you and the story of our people will come into your memory. It's quite wonderful."

"How could that be?"

"Over the years, for very many years, one of the elders would keep the Memory Stick, and if something important happened, he would scribe marks into the stick, so that it would remember. Those who were trained could coax the stick to tell the story just by touching those marks in a certain way. It was our whole history from earliest times."

"You're forgetting the fire, Grandma," Mama-Q said.

"Fire?" Little-Q asked.

"Yes," Grandma said. "Part of our history was lost when they started to burn the Memory Stick. Hero-Q saved it, and that's what was handed down."

"Where is the Memory Stick now, Grandma? I'll get it for you."

"No one has seen it since the people ran from the Wash..." For a moment she was lost in remembrance. "Enough of this. You have to be up early tomorrow!"

"Yes, Little-Q," Mama-Q said. "That's enough for tonight."

Papa-Q did not return that day or the next day or the days after that, and as the days went on and he did not return, the work at the Tall Pole continued for Little-Q.

He liked being at the Tall Pole with Grandpa, but not what he went through to get there.

It meant rising in the darkness and trotting behind Grandpa down the path where the darkness was so deep and scary, and hearing all those strange night sounds. That frightening screech could be the call of an owl, or it might be some other creature of the dark that he had been warned about. Anyone of them might attack him or carry him off —or worse.

At the Pole, he would wait alone as Grandpa went to the edge of the world. Little-Q tried to be alert, although a part of him always wanted to go back to sleep, even as he stood.

A sudden sound from Grandpa brought him broad awake.

What was it? Little-Q was not sure. Was it a call or a greeting or something else? It sounded like singing, a coaxing song. Then a call.

Suddenly, the first response from Mr. Sun would strike him. That first arrow of brilliance always caught him by surprise. Little-Q watched for its trace on the Great Stone, ready to make his mark.

When Grandpa came and examined his work, he would talk about what they were doing.

"You see," Grandpa said one morning as he paced back and forth around the stone, "this place is ideal for the work. We can see right to the very edge of the world and even beyond. That is most important."

He made a sweeping gesture toward the outline, which was stark against the horizon.

"Look there! You can see every detail of the Old Man of the Mountain out there! You see?"

Little-Q nodded and looked for the points which Grandpa knew so well.

Grandpa saw his doubting look. "You may not see it all now. You will. When you come into the knowledge, many things will be made clear to you. You simply do not need it right now, so you are not aware. Don't worry. You will see. You will."

He pointed to the stone. "Here. You see where we mark where Mr. Sun comes to us? Important! You are doing important work!"

Some days Grandpa worried about "things moving too fast" and would ask Little-Q if he was sure—"Really sure!"—that his marks were right on the sighting. Little-Q assured him, as best he could, but Grandpa checked and double-checked.

To Little-Q the marks on the Great Stone were merely a series of scratches. The pattern was interesting, but it did not make sense to him.

"Never mind!" Grandpa reassured him. "It will come around for you one of these days. When you are ready."

"Maybe when I'm named, I'll understand?" Little-Q asked.

"Before then! No ceremony can do that for you, give you understanding. You see, the thing itself—the naming—doesn't change you. It's because you are changed that you are given your name."

"Changed?"

"Yes, changed. I'm not sure I can explain it." Grandpa was thoughtful a moment. He was struck by an idea. "There! That's it!"

"What is it, Grandpa?"

"When you were in your egg, everything that was you was in there, just waiting to come out. To anyone who looked, you were just an ordinary egg. When you were ready, you came out –a beautiful creature —and you were given a family name. Now, the real you is inside you, waiting for the right moment..."

"I don't think I understand."

Grandpa waited for Little-Q to stash the marking stick. When they started down the path, he said seriously, "It's too bad your father is not here to teach you these things. You are having to grow up very quickly. That's all right. You can do it. We expect great things from you. Great things."

"What do you mean, Grandpa?"

"I expect you will become one of our great guides," he said easily. "Perhaps like Hero-Q."

Little-Q was startled. "I don't know about that!"

"Of course not. Not now. You are still a child, spending your days playing children's games. Soon—soon!—things that are hidden will suddenly become clear. You will be able to do things you never expected. Or even knew about."

During the day, Little-Q returned to his friends and the covey games. One afternoon, playing Run-Q-Run, he and Cousin-Q ran to hide in the cover of tall grass and scraggly brush near the Tall Pole. Cousin-Q had never been this close to the pole and he cautioned Little-Q.

"I don't think we should be here," he said with a worried tone. "If anyone sees us, we could be in deep trouble."

Little-Q reassured him: "I come out here all the time with my grandpa."

"Yes, but that's different."

Little-Q had an impulse to show Cousin-Q the Great Stone and tell him about his work with Grandpa. "It's okay. I want to show you something. Come on."

Little-Q started to trot closer to the pole.

Cousin-Q held back. "I don't think we should."

"It's okay, I told you."

Cousin-Q looked up at the pole and noticed a movement beyond it in the sky.

"There's Hawk," he said. "I wonder if he's looking at us."

Little-Q glanced at the easy circling of the widespread wings outlined against a bank of gathering clouds. "We're all right. He's way over there."

As he went closer to the pole, Little-Q had second thoughts about showing off his work. He felt that he should keep a little distance from the pole and the record of his marks.

Cousin-Q stepped back cautiously. "Little-Q! I told you!"

More clouds gathered above them, darkening the sky. The sunlight disappeared and the air became suddenly cool.

"I don't think we should be here," Cousin-Q protested.

Even though he had doubts, Little-Q impulsively approached the pole. There was a peculiar quality there, which he could not explain and wanted to ignore. Some unseen energy surrounded the pole, as if protecting it from intrusion. Cousin-Q felt it too.

Now that he had brought Cousin-Q this far, he had to show him something. Little-Q turned and went to the cache of the Marking Stick.

"Here's really something!" he said. "Let me show you this!"

He pulled out the Marking Stick. As he held the stick, it quivered in his hand. He did not feel a movement like this when he was using the stick for his work with Grandpa.

"Here, take it," Little-Q said, offering it to Cousin-Q.

Cousin-Q took it tentatively. "What is it? Hey! It feels funny! You'd better put it back."

"It would make a good throwing-stick."

"I don't like it," Cousin-Q said, backing away. "Here." He tossed the stick to Little-Q.

Little-Q caught the stick, held it a moment, tightening his grip against its quiver, and threw it to Cousin-Q. "Here it comes again!"

"No!" Cousin-Q was frightened. He caught the stick and quickly threw it back to Little-Q.

Little-Q caught it just as a bolt of lightning flashed nearby and a great rolling boom of thunder crashed through the air. The ground trembled beneath their feet just as the stick vibrated when they held it. The air was filled with the smell of lightning and a sudden shower of rain.

"Wow!" Little-Q shouted. "We'd better run for it!"

He quickly put the Marking Stick back in its place and, as the sudden storm pelted their backs with big wet drops, they ran for the ditch. They huddled under an old cotton-wood whose roots spread into the ditch in a way that created shelter from the

"Wow!" Cousin-Q said. "I told you!"

"We'll be all right here for a while," Little-Q said. He did not feel as brave as his words. Was their Marking Stick play connected with the earth-shaking thunder and sudden rain?

A dark shape farther down the ditch caught his eye. The figure looked familiar. It couldn't be!

"Quinata?" he asked.

The figure raised its head against the rain. It was Quinata, princess from the covey to the north.

CHAPTER 7

Quinata made herself smaller, trying to avoid the rain and the two intruders. Little-Q went to her.

"Is that you?" he asked.

She nodded, then shook her head to send him away. "Please go and leave us alone."

"What happened to you? He asked, rain running off his head and down his back.

"You don't understand." The rain on Quinata's face added to her tears of hurt and defeat. "Please go away."

"No. You're hurt. You need help."

"Thank you, but we do not need help." The words reminded her of her mission. She straightened and spoke more directly: "We want to pass through your land."

"What has happened? Are there others with you?"

She turned her head slightly, indicating other shadowy forms huddled in the dark wet. "Please. Let us go through."

Cousin-Q joined them. "Who is it? That girl who came before? The false alarm? It looks like her."

"Never mind that now," Little-Q said to him. "This is no false alarm." Turning to Quinata, he asked: "Your father, does he know you're here?"

A shudder passed through Quinata, disturbing the rivulets of raindrops on her feathers. "He's... he's ...back there."

Her effort at bravery broke a little. "With my mother. And many others."

Little-Q groaned. "They did attack, after all."

She nodded. "It was terrible. We are going to a new place in the south. We've heard that it's safe there."

"Moving south!" Little-Q objected. "No! You'll stay here. I'll speak to Grandpa. He'll want you to."

Quinata shook her head again. "No, he will remember me like this one she indicated Cousin-Q"—as the one who brought the false alarm and frightened everyone when there was nothing to be frightened—" She gave in and the tears came. "Now it's all so real and so terrible."

The rain had eased to a sprinkle and as they talked it stopped altogether.

"Come with us," Little-Q said. "At least let us give you something to eat."

Quinata raised her head and, with a deep breath, shook off the tears. "We do need food and rest."

As they came out of the ditch, Little-Q looked up at the sky, where a ray of sunshine broke through the clouds.

"Look!" he called out. "Mr. Sun is back! I know that everything is going to be all right!"

At the mention of Mr. Sun, Quinata looked at Little-Q with a puzzled expression, as if to say, "You know him that well?" but she said nothing.

Little-Q and Cousin-Q led Quinata and her small band of people away from the ditch.

At the stable area, the refugees ate and watered eagerly. Little-Q ran to find Grandpa-Q, who quickly came with Uncle-Q and the elders. Others of the covey gathered in concern for Quinata and her people.

Quinata said that the monsters attacked at first light. After lying dormant for so long, no one expected them to suddenly come to life. When they did arouse, they swept across the land, stripping off everything of value. They went on all day, destroying trees and buildings, scraping away sage and grass.

"How terrible!" someone in the crowd gasped. "It's a plague."

"Was there no sign—no warning?"

"Perhaps," Quinata said. "Some remarked on the blossoming of small yellow flowers on our land before the attack. We had not seen these peculiar plants before."

The mention of "yellow flowers" was taken up in the crowd.

"We've had those!"

"We thought they were poison, but they weren't."

"We pulled them up."

"Quiet, please!" Grandpa commanded. "Let her finish."

Quinata said that when the monsters began moving about, brave warriors rushed to stop them and many were lost in the futile counterattack. Quinata's father was one of those hurt. He could not travel, so her mother stayed to care for him. She suffered terrible injuries, too.

"We must find a new place to live," she said. "We've heard that it's safe south of the water. After we rest, we'll be on our way."

"Nonsense!" Grandpa said. "You'll stay here."

"Yes," Uncle-Q put in. "We are safe here. We have food and water, shelter for our nests. Plenty of room for new people."

"Yes, and welcome, too!" Grandpa insisted. "We must send scouts back to your land to help others come to us."

Some of the women asked Quinata to go with them to rest.

"You've had a hard journey."

"No," Quinata said. "I must be sure that my people are taken care of."

Grandpa asked Uncle-Q to get a rescue party organized.

"Yes, good," Uncle-Q said, then to the crowd: "Call for scouts!"

Several men immediately stepped forward. Pushing their way to the front of the group were a half dozen young ones, all calling, "Me! I'll go! Me!"

"Quiet!" Uncle-Q commanded. "We can't take children!"

"Wait a minute," someone objected. "It might be a good idea to train a new crop of scouts. Let's take a few."

"All right," Uncle said, looking around. "We must be very selective about this. What we have to do won't be easy."

Little-Q started forward, hoping to be chosen, but his mother's touch on his shoulder stopped him. He looked up with a "Why not?" question in his eyes.

She shook her head, and he fell back with a groan of disappointment.

Those around them did not notice as Mama-Q and Little-Q eased their way to the back of the crowd.

"Remember," she said, "it's an honor to work with Grandpa every day. His name is known everywhere among our people. Everyone depends on him—and his helper. You'll realize that someday."

"I could be back in time."

"Maybe. Maybe not. Grandpa needs you."

She rubbed the back feathers between his shoulder blades comfortingly. "It's much more important than being a scout for one day. I think if your papa were here, he'd say that sometimes you have to give up what you want to do for what you have to do."

Quinata told Grandpa that she appreciated the offer of assistance to her people.

"I can see that you have much room and lots of food and water," she said. "I wonder, though—what if something should happen and you had to leave this place?"

Grandpa hurried to reassure her: "We have another place over there, across the water."

She wanted to see it, just to make sure.

"I'm needed here, but—" Grandpa lifted a gesture toward the back of the group. "Would you, Little-Q?"

Quinata and Little-Q were on the path that led to the crossing over the water when Cousin-Q passed them in a rush.

"I'm going!" he called. "My dad said I can go! As soon as I tell my mom!"

Quinata stopped and remarked that Cousin-Q must be going with the rescue party to her land in the north. Little-Q grunted.

He guessed so.

She looked at him sideways. "Perhaps you have also volunteered and I am delaying you."

Little-Q answered with an unintelligible grunt.

"I would want to go," she said, "but I was sent here to find a new place."

He did not respond.

Her questioning look said, "Too busy with children's games?"

He felt a heavy weight of frustration that made his insides hard.

She saw that he was sensitive to the subject. "I'm sorry. My remarks were not proper for one who is a guest."

They heard a call from the canal below. Little-Q was happy for the distraction. A duck was paddling in the easy-flowing water.

"This is most embarrassing," Duck said, "but I must ask. Have you seen any of my people?"

The question was unexpected. Here was one of the great family of travelers—usually seen only at the highest places in the sky, flying in beautiful formation and singing exuberantly—on the land of the Covey, on a narrow sprit of water in the desert.

Little-Q smiled in disbelief. "You are lost?"

Duck rose up and splashed water with beating wings. "Of course not! But my people are. We were separated in the darkness"

"So you ended up here," Quinata said.

"I was blown off course. That's the only way to account for it. This tiny stream was the only water I could find."

"It must be frightening to be off all by yourself."

"It is my first trip, but I'm sure we'll get together soon," Duck said. "Where are you folks from?"

"We live here. We have food enough the year around."

"You must try a vacation in the south sometime. There's something special about getting there. You are up so high, with the moon over your shoulder and the flying is easy and the whole group singing and... It's a thrill."

"It does look like fun. What happened to you?"

"I got careless, I'm afraid. Something distracted me. Perhaps I dozed off during a quiet time. The next thing I know I dropped away, and they were all out of sight."

Quinata said, "The weather is so warm, it seems early to be moving south."

"We left cold," Duck said, "Cold is coming to you here."

"That's what my grandfather says," Little-Q said. "Mr. Sun is going back—"

When he interrupted himself, Quinata looked at him sharply.

Cousin-Q ran past them toward the stables.

"I'm a scout!" he called out. "See you later!"

"We'd better go," Quinata said.

"Yes," Little-Q said, adding to Duck: "Good luck in your travels."

"Thank you," Duck said.

At Uncle-Q's place, Aunt-Q shook her head over Cousin-Q's sudden independence.

"He didn't even ask my permission," she said. "He said his father approved and he only came to tell me he's going. Part of growing up, I'm afraid." She spoke to Little-Q: "Of course, you won't be going, will you. What a relief for your mother." She turned back to Quinata. "Let me show you around."

They were in a small place crowded with grass and ragged bushes and metal devices.

"I notice that you're fenced in," Quinata said.

"No, no," Aunt-Q objected. "We are not fenced in. They are fenced out and we are safe."

"You certainly have a lot of grass."

"Yes, isn't it wonderful! There's always something to snack on. Some say we're overgrown, but we don't mind. We have plenty to share."

They moved around the place.

"Of course, for our heavy meals, we go across the water and eat with the others. My husband has always liked it here. The quiet—"

At that moment, a loud humming noise started up from a large device in the center of the enclosure. A great spurt of water began to splash from a curved pipe into a straight pipe.

Quinata was startled. "That noise! What is it?"

"Don't mind that," Aunt-Q shouted. "You get used to it. In fact, it's rather soothing after a while."

As they were getting ready to leave, Quinata remarked, "Yes, it's very nice, but I wonder if there would be enough nesting for all of us."

"I don't think we have to worry about that now," Aunt-Q reassured her.

At the path, Little-Q began to go the way they came. Quinata asked about the other direction.

"Where does this go?" she asked, indicating the opposite track.

"No place, " Little-Q said. "We never go there."

"I'd like to see."

Reluctantly, Little-Q turned. "All right. I'll show you."

He stepped onto the narrow pathway which barely showed between scraggly plants. He and Quinata went slowly. She asked about Grandpa-Q.

"He's fine."

"He looked rather tired when I saw him today."

"I don't think so."

"Perhaps you don't notice because you see him every day."

Little-Q thought she was sure the wise one about all sorts of things. He said, "He's all right."

"My father mentions him from time to time. He is very well known throughout all the coveys. For his work and his wisdom."

"He's mostly Grandpa to us."

When they neared the curve of the path, Little-Q stopped and looked toward the end of the world. This was where he said good-bye to Papa-Q. Quinata watched him silently. Did she see tears in his eyes?

"This is as far as we go," he said.

"What's out there?"

"A long time ago, our people used to live in what they call the Wash. Then the water came and they had to move and they lost everything. I've never seen it. This is the end of our land."

"Why haven't you gone out there?"

"Papa stopped me here."

"He went to the unknown lands?"

"Yes. Can you see that star, there against the cloud?"

"It's unusual to see a star at a time like this..."

"Papa used it to guide on. It's at the very end of the world."

"Yes, I can see it now. Against the clouds."

"No one goes out there, unless they have to."

"Like your Papa?" Quinata guessed.

"Yes." A glint of color caught his eye. "Look! It's raining!"

"It must be the rain that we had."

"Maybe we'll see a rainbow!" The idea lifted Little-Q's spirits.

Quinata was silent a moment, then: "I am sorry, Little-Q. I misjudged you. Since your father left, you must be the one working with—"

He interrupted. "We don't talk about that."

"It must be very special to be with Qwa-Say-Qua at that time. To do the Work."

"Let's not talk about it."

Perhaps Quinata was trying to move away from her apology to new ground, when she said, "My father says there has been some debate recently about the Work. Some believe it is old-fashioned and out-of-date."

Little-Q turned to her. "What my grandfather does is important to the whole world! Everybody knows that!"

"Yes, I believe that, too," she said quickly. "My father says that in the long run, history will decide."

"I'm not sure what you're talking about, but my grandpa is all right," Little-Q said. He pointed excitedly. "Look! A rainbow! Out there!"

"It's beautiful," she said.

"It's a good sign. I'm sure it's a good sign."

They looked at it a few moments in silence.

Little-Q thought that sometimes this girl from the north made good sense when she talked. He was beginning to feel something toward Quinata that he could not explain. He could actually feel her standing beside him, without their even touching. He knew that if they did touch, he would feel a vibration. Like the one with the marking stick, but a good vibration, not scary. What's going on here? he wondered.

When they turned back toward the land, they saw dust rising into the air over the corral.

"Is that what you call a dust devil?" Quinata asked.

"I'm afraid it's something worse!" Little-Q said.

CHAPTER 8

The stable area was a place of panic. Everyone was running every which way. As Little-Q and Quinata tried to make sense of what was going on, someone ran by and scolded them for not being alarmed.

"Don't you see! The yellow flowers! They're back! Bigger than ever!"

These were different from all the other flowers. Their woody stalk was tall and skinny. They had no fragrance and no green leaves. Their flowers were thin with a shiny texture and hung down, and moved in the breeze.

Another shouted: "The baby monster came and planted them all over! It's the end of us for sure!"

In the confusion of milling people, a straight, calm figure walked to the center of the corral, where a flat yellow blossom stood on a skinny stiff stalk. It was Old Quaymon. His slow-moving, stiff-backed presence stood out in the center of the storm of panic.

"Look! Look at Old Quaymon!"

The covey people stopped to watch. He went to the flower, looked at it calmly for a moment, then touched it gingerly.

Old Quaymon leaned over and pecked with more assurance. The flat yellow flower moved a bit on its stalk, as if a slight breeze brushed it.

Old Quaymon looked around in a show of confidence. He leaned over the flower, nipped tentatively. Another nip, more vigorous.

Some people gasped. "He'll be killed."

Others said No, they aren't poison. We know that.

But these are bigger, more yellow.

We got rid of them before.

So many this time! They're different.

Old Quaymon is taking an awful chance.

"Wait," a calmer voice put in. "Let's see what happens."

Old Quaymon leaned over the flower again, taking it well into his beak.

Nothing happened.

He gripped the blossom and pulled, as if taking an insect out of the ground. His pull moved the skinny stalk. Old Quaymon let go, took a deep breath, gripped more strongly and pulled with all his weight. The flower slipped out of the ground. Old Quaymon was thrown onto his back, mouth open in surprise.

The flower flew away from him and the people backed off away its fall. Recovering from their surprise, they looked back at Old Quaymon, who was struggling to get up, and laughed. His heroism turned into comedy. The yellow flower had again lost its terrible spell.

Recovering, Old Quaymon went to the flower. He picked it up, shook it sharply, and dropped it.

He looked up with triumph. "See! I'm fine! Even this larger one is nothing!"

He took the thing in his beak, walked to the edge of the corral, dropped it in loose dirt, and scratched a little earth over it.

When he went back to the center of the corral, the people ran out to make sure he was all right, laughing and shouting. Soon, others were testing flowers around the corral and stable area, pecking at them and trying to pull them out of the ground. Some were successful.

Near the big stump, Grandpa watched with a grave, worried expression.

"I don't like this," he said.

"I know what you mean," Quinata, who was close by, answered. "It was not a joke when these were on our land."

"They may be dangerous in ways we do not suppose. I'm afraid of what might happen now."

Old Quaymon came over and heard the exchange.

"Relax, old man!" he said loudly. "Can't you see that it's nothing to be worried about? We'll be fine."

"I'm not so sure," Grandpa-Q said. "That was a crazy thing to do, you know. These are so much larger."

Old Quaymon came close and turned so that only Grandpa could hear: "I know. I was scared to death."

"Then why—!"

"I don't like to see our people put into such a fright by a thing like that. I guess I wanted to show a little of our covey's spirit, like the old days."

"Then it was a very brave thing you did."

"We have to decide what this means and what we should do about it."

Everyone asked the same question, and the debate went on all morning and through loafing time.

They remembered that when flowers like these appeared on covey land before, nothing happened. So nothing would happen now. Especially since Old Quaymon showed that these were harmless too, even if they were so much larger.

Others said, "Remember the attack on the land to the north, where Quinata's people lost everything."

"The monsters came right after the yellow flowers," they said.

"We will have to fight!"

"It's useless to try to stop them," Quinata said. "They are so big, so powerful. Our best warriors could not stop them. Worse, they were killed outright or hurt very badly."

"What will we do?"

"It is not pleasant to think about, since we have a tradition of bravery," Grandpa said, "but I think we will simply have to run for safety."

"That's cowardly."

"We must keep the covey together," Grandpa said. "We must have a place for Quinata's people and our scouts to come back to. We must."

The last word came from one who was hungry: "We're all right for now. Let's eat."

When they were alone, Little-Q asked Grandpa what he thought would happen.

Grandpa looked very serious. He touched Little-Q's shoulder and said:

"I think we will have to find another place to live."

"You mean we will have to move?"

"Yes, sad to say. Our people have moved before."

"But the Tall Pole..."

"We have to go on with the work. We must not stop the work. So much has been done. We can It lose that."

Little-Q realized that he meant not only the Tall Pole but also the Great Stone and its markings. The people could move, I but how could they move the Pole and the Great Stone?

It was an uneasy night for the covey. Little-Q felt that he never slept, but was awake all night, thinking about what might happen. Suddenly, Mama-Q was shaking him and whispering, "Little-Q! It's time."

When Little-Q was with Grandpa at the Tall Pole, he liked being part of the change from the darkness to light.

"This is our time," he thought. "Just me and Grandpa. Everybody else asleep."

He absorbed the cool quiet through his feather-ends. He gazed up at the hero-stars. "Our people. My people."

He noticed that the stars faded when the struggle began between darkness and light beyond the Old Man of the Mountain. He wondered what became of those stars. Where they went. Perhaps it was told on the Memory Stick.

"What will happen to us?" he wondered. He touched the pole, felt its cool solidity, and looked down at the Great Stone, still in a dark shadow. 'How can we ever move away?'

Little-Q gripped the marking-stick. He stood ready.

"Whatever happens," he said aloud, as if making a vow to the hero-stars, "we have to stay with the work!"

At the moment when he felt he could not wait any longer. "What's taking so long?"—he heard Grandpa call out. The first streak of light from Mr. Sun struck him and he saw the shadow of the Tall Pole fall across the Great Stone.

Decisively, with the assurance that comes with experience, he made his mark. In a few moments, Grandpa ran up, looked approvingly, and clapped him on the back. "Good! Very good! It's coming along. There is something..."

Grandpa walked around the stone. At one point, he stopped, rubbed his chin thoughtfully, and indicated one series of marks. "Perhaps coming along too quickly. An unusual time."

He motioned to Little-Q to come look. "See here?" he pointed. "Are you sure you marked it right?"

Little-Q assured him: "I've been very careful."

"Yes, of course. I'm sure you have. It's a pattern I hadn't noticed. It has never done this. It's all moving too quickly."

Grandpa shivered, as if a cold-wind passed through and touched him.

Little-Q looked at the marks and nodded, but did not quite understand. He did not ask, because he was sure that Grandpa would say that he will understand when he was "ready."

More important, there were other questions on his mind — what the covey was going to do, and what would happened with the Tall Pole. He felt more responsible now.

He wanted to make a suggestion, perhaps to show that he was really growing up and getting away from games and could be taken seriously. But he did not know what to suggest.

Grandpa straightened up. "Altogether, Little-Q, we are living in a very unusual time. Very unusual."

Little-Q felt somehow better when he heard Grandpa say right out loud the same uncertainty he felt: "I wonder what it all means." After a pause, Grandpa added, "We can't decide today."

Standing side by side, they felt the warmth of Mr. Sun spreading over the land before them. The light reached as far as the Day Star at the very end of the world, glinting a greeting, it seemed, back to them.

"Isn't it beautiful?" Grandpa said. "Doesn't it make you feel good about the work?"

Suddenly, he grasped Little-Q sharply and pointed.

"Look! What's that?"

Before them, over the covey land at the stable and corral, waves of dust were rising in swirling, ominous clouds that darkly reflected the first light.

They ran.

Big yellow monsters—machines as big as the stable building—were carousing brutally on the covey land. They swept this way and that, knocking down the fences, pulling over the trees, scraping away the brush and grass, throwing rocks and dirt and chunks of wreckage into the air.

In the first sweep, as they invaded the land, the monsters struck the nesting area along the fence line. Scraping away everything, they moved at will.

"Fortunately," someone explained to Grandpa later, "no one was there."

The people had left their nests for breakfast. Many were in the stable.

The only warning was the loud roar as the monsters approached. The noise alone was frightening. The persistent, unstoppable scraping heaviness of their movements added to the terror.

At first, those feeding in the stable were more interested in going on with their meal than dealing with the sudden noise outside.

When part of one wall of the stable came away, exposing the covey people to the light and air, it seemed so unnatural that many stood there, reacting as spectators, instead of responding to the danger.

Others, acting on instinct, tried to fly to safety, but they were caught inside the building. Then in a rush, most ran out and got away as best they could.

Through the rising dirt cloud, Grandpa and Little-Q saw only chaos. The only way clear was toward the water.

"Run for it!" someone shouted at them. "Save yourselves!"

"Get away from the stable! The stable is the worst!"

"What shall we do? Where can we go?"

"Across the water!" Grandpa shouted.

Through the dust and noise and confusion Grandpa sensed that the monsters moved with a certain rhythm.

"Everyone go! Quickly!" Grandpa ordered. "Before the next sweep!"

Then, to Little-Q, he urged, "Come on! Let's see what we can do!"

He and Little-Q were able to move between the sweeps to make their way toward the wreckage of the stable. Some of the covey were still there, hiding in fright in corners of the battered building.

Grandpa and Little-Q and others who were not hurt helped the people to the crossing of the water.

"Get everyone to the other side. We'll be safe there. If only for a while."

Suddenly, the attack stopped. The monsters rested, heaving and smoking and ruminating their meal of stable planks, corral rails, trees, rocks and bushes.

Taking advantage of this time, the covey slipped away, actually moving in the shadow of some of the monsters, toward the crossing over the water.

They ran onto the crossing and to the other side, where they came together in small groups, searching for family and friends.

"It's a miracle that we got away!"

"That more weren't hurt!"

They crowded into Uncle-Q's place.

"We ought to send someone back to see if anybody got left behind!"

"We checked as best we could, and got everyone out that we could find."

Grandpa went slowly from one family to another. For each he had a touch and a word of encouragement and comfort. He was not himself, and appeared to be carrying an injury of some kind. Grandma-Q came to him.

"What is it?" she asked quietly. "Are you hurt?"

"I'm all right. It's just that—the yellow monsters on our land—I feel so responsible."

"How could you possibly?"

Others nearby heard and joined in.

"It couldn't be your fault, Grandpa!"

"You had nothing to do with the attack."

"I was not alert and we were not ready," he said. "Worse, I sent the scouts out, and we were left unprotected."

Quinata spoke up: "It would not have done any good. When the attack came on our land, our best people were lost. What you did actually meant that your scouts were not here. They could not do anything foolish and perhaps be injured or, worse, killed outright. No one can stop the yellow monsters."

Grandpa did not seem convinced. He shook his head slowly and sadly. "They tricked us with that false alarm strategy. I didn't see it. I let you down."

This was protested immediately with strong shouts of "No!" "No!"

"If it's anyone's fault," Quinata said, "it is mine—for coming here and leading the monsters to your land, and then allowing you to send your scouts back to my land. I am the one who should be faulted."

"No, Quinata," Old Quaymon said. "What has happened is not your fault. The monsters attacked both of us without any reason at all and destroyed all of our homes."

Others joined in, assuring Grandpa and Quinata that they could not be blamed for what happened.

Grandpa's pain was not eased. Later Little-Q would see that from this time, Grandpa began to be, somehow, different: not as strong with Mr. Sun or as excited about the Old Man of the Mountain or as particular about the marks on the Great Stone as he was used to seeing him every morning at the pole.

One of the elders standing nearby tried to encourage Grandpa.

"Don't worry, old man," he said. "We're safe here. After the monsters eat their fill, they will move on. We will have the place to ourselves again. Just like what happened with the horses. They tore things up—those big feet were really scary!—but one day, they were gone. This will be the same, and we'll go back."

"We've never seen anything as bad as this," Grandpa said. "No, as much as I would like to agree with you, I don't think it's going to work that way."

Uncle-Q pointed at the dust that was rising again over the corral. "Before they go away, they're going to scrape it clean."

"Sad, isn't it?" Grandpa said. "It's happening to us just like one of the stories on the Memory Stick."

"I do hope this arrangement is temporary," Aunt-Q said. "You have my sympathy, but this is more than I ever expected. Now you'll find out what it means to live on the other side of the water."

CHAPTER 9

The Tall Pole survived, along with a patch of green nearby. This was where they had stashed the marking stick, which was, miraculously, undisturbed.

"No one was up here for them to run after," Grandpa said.

To reach the Pole now, Grandpa and Little-Q had to cross the water, a frightening hazard in the dark. Once at the Pole, Little-Q found that this was the best part of the day. The air smelled clean and clear and cool – chill now that Mr. Sun let the cold approach—and it was good to be away even for a little time from the crowd at Aunt-Q's.

Little-Q thought he noticed that Grandpa seemed somewhat older and weaker, but he was faithful to the Pole and the Great Stone. From the high place of the Pole, in the first light after their work, Grandpa and Little-Q could look over the covey land. It was bare and smoothed over unnaturally. It had lain silent and untouched since the day of the attack.

"Mama wonders why they went to all that trouble," Little-Q said one morning.

"It's the way of the dark!" Grandpa said angrily. "It attacks and destroys. It's been going on a long time. I'm afraid this is not the end of it."

"What's happening to us, Grandpa?"

"Don't you see!" he said sharply. "The chaos comes out of the dark and—"

Little-Q flinched at this sudden, impatient scold. Grandpa saw this and softened.

"I'm sorry. You have no way of knowing. You haven't been taught. You've never heard the Memory Stick sing."

After a silence, Grandpa seemed to be talking to himself when he said, "Perhaps if I was more vigilant. Or did something different..."

The ugliness before them brought up a feeling of anger and determination in Little-Q. The land which was so spacious as the home of the Q-Covey now was such a small, bare place. The field where he played run-Q-run and stick throwing games in tall grass and brush was now stripped and leveled. He remembered Grackle's scream: "You are doomed! Doomed!"

"We aren't doomed," he said aloud. "We just have to find a new place to live, that's all."

"What was that?" Grandpa asked.

"Mama says that we'll probably have to migrate. Maybe not migrate exactly."

"Find a new place to live. Yes, I think she's right. There's nothing here for us, is there? There are too many of us crowded into your uncle's place."

Grandpa-Q seemed in pain. It was as if the attack of the yellow monsters had wounded him physically, but he did not want it to show. Grandpa noticed Little-Q looking at him and added: "I'll be all right. Perhaps the scouts will bring news. We must do something soon."

"What about the Pole?"

"—and the Great Stone," Grandpa said solemnly. "I'm not sure what to do. What we can do. Our work is here."

"If we move —move away from the Pole —"

"We must be faithful to the work. So much depends on it. Yes, we must."

"Maybe we should just live here. You and me. Live at the Pole."

"I've been thinking about that," Grandpa looked around at the small clutch of growth near the pole. "We probably couldn't make it through the cold with the place picked clean like this. Such an abundance—now gone! Besides, having someone here might provoke the monsters into coming back."

Little-Q put away the marking-stick, and Grandpa suggested they try to find some breakfast before going back to the crowd at Uncle-Q's. Coming down from the Pole, they heard voices in the ditch and discovered the party of scouts had returned and taken cover there.

The scouts had traveled during the dark, bringing the last refugees from the north. They'd found their land strangely barren. Everything they were familiar with had been wiped away in the attack. They'd stopped in the ditch to wait for full light.

When they saw Grandpa and Little-Q, they could not believe that they were on the land of the Q-Covey. Then they were all talking at once, each trying to learn what happened here and what the scouts went through in the north.

They were silenced when a plaintive voice from the back called out: "I'm hungry!"

Grandpa asked Little-Q to guide the refugees to the crossing of the water, and over to Uncle-Q's place.

When Little-Q moved out, he noticed that Cousin-Q stayed with the men. On the way, Little-Q learned that the scouting party had run into trouble. Bad trouble. Something about the monsters and the dark. Little-Q could not make out exactly what happened, but it was clear that Cousin-Q had saved Uncle-Q's life.

"Pulled him out of the way in just the nick of time," he was told. "Not the width of a feather between him and that awful thing!"

Little-Q started to say, "Why that means — -" He stopped himself, because now he understood why Cousin-Q had earned his position with the men. While he was glad for Cousin-Q, he thought that if he had gone to the land to the north, he might have done something heroic, too.

"Don't worry," Mama-Q told him later. "Your time will come. For now, helping at the Pole is heroic enough."

It was not until they reached Uncle-Q's place that Little-Q learned that in the new attack on the land in the north, Quinata's mother and father were lost, along with several others.

What everyone hoped would be a joyful coming together of family members became instead a time of mourning.

Aunt-Q and other women of the Q-Covey welcomed the newcomers and comforted them as best they could. Everyone was scrupulously kind, but the crowding became worse and put tempers on edge.

Grandpa, the elders, and the scouts got together to assess the damage. They compared what the scouts saw to the north with what happened to the land of the Q-Covey. The results were the same: Everything was stripped away. The destruction was complete in both places.

"Perhaps other places as well," Uncle-Q said. "The attacks are sweeping south in a regular pattern."

Grandpa kept blaming himself, but everyone agreed that there was nothing that could have been done. The concern now was simply to survive with what was left.

"So many eating," one said, "and the cold coming on..."

They asked Grandpa about the cold.

"It's coming on fast," he said. "I'm afraid the water from the sky may make things worse this time."

"I just wish Papa-Q would come back," Uncle-Q said. "He might have news for us about a new place to live."

Someone else said, "Yes, we need a new place."

Later, the two coveys came together for a solemn Memorial Service. Grandpa spoke.

In the distance behind Grandpa, Little-Q noticed Grackle pacing up and down. He pecked at the ground, and then pointed his sharp beak at the service, looking and listening.

"Old busy-body," Little-Q thought. "He'll rub it in now."

"Once again the dark sends out its army of chaos," Grandpa was saying, "to attack and destroy..."

Little-Q didn't hear it all; he was watching Cousin-Q, who stood with his father. He looked different. He was different now. He took his position with the elders and other men in the front during the service. Someday, perhaps.

"From earliest times, the Memory Stick tells us..."

Little-Q noticed that even before the service, Grandpa was not himself. He lacked his old strength. He was content to find a place in the shade and suggest to others that they run here or run there and report back to him. They did so gladly, because they respected his knowledge and experience and his judgment, which had guided the covey for so long.

"...But now..." Grandpa was saying as the service concluded, "but now—"

His voice trailed off, and the people wondered if he could continue. He straightened, pulled a deep breath into his chest and raised his head, so that his topknot was silhouetted against the sky. "We must keep on. Even in our sadness and discouragement and losses—we must. So much depends on us."

After the service, Quinata and her remnant went with the women of the Q-Covey. The men stood around talking, remembering better times, speculating about the future. The younger ones scattered. "Not too far!" they were warned.

Cousin-Q came up to Little-Q, asking if he wanted to "go somewhere and do something." He had a sheepish look, which tried to conceal how deep down proud he was now that he was accepted by the Elders.

"Sure," Little-Q said. "Don't you want to stay with them?"

"All they do is stand around and talk. I've got to loosen up. You know, run around a little."

"That's a good idea. Let's get out of here, anyway."

They went out to the stretch of green growth between the Uncle-Q's place and the path beside the water. Little-Q found a good throwing stick, and they began to pitch it back and forth.

Just when they were getting a good rhythm, they heard a scolding voice:

"Be careful there!" The men had come out of Uncle-Q's place, too.

"We were here first," Cousin-Q said to Little-Q. "Come on, throw me a long one!"

Little-Q stepped back and threw. The stick went wide and into some tall grass and weeds by the fence. Cousin-Q ran to pick it up.

"Hey, here's a better one!" he called, holding up a new stick.

He threw it to Little-Q, who caught it easily and hefted it.

"Yeah, this is a good one!"

The stick had bumps, which gave him a good grip. One end was charred, the rest well weathered or perhaps rubbed.

Little-Q prepared to throw. "This one is a lot better!"

The stick felt light, wanting to fly on its own. Little-Q lifted it back over his shoulder and with an expert flick, let it go.

The stick flew in a curve that sent it toward the men. It fluttered and wavered. With an unexpected spin, it lowered and turned, went into the group and struck Grandpa on the shoulder.

He looked at his shoulder, then at the stick on the ground, and frowned angrily at Little-Q.

"I'm sorry, Grandpa!" Little-Q called out, running forward.

Grandpa felt his shoulder. "I'm not hurt. You kids ought to be more careful."

He picked up the stick, prepared to toss it to Little-Q. He stopped and gripped it more firmly. "That's funny. You've got a most unusual stick here. Wait..."

He looked at it carefully, turning it slowly. "Is it possible! Look at this! Am I right... ?"

He handed the stick to Uncle-Q.

"What do you think?"

Uncle-Q held it and looked. "It is unusual."

The stick was handed to another. "Maybe left behind by somebody."

"Or thrown away," the next one said. "It's been burned."

"Nothing special. Give it back to the kids."

"No, no! " Grandpa insisted. "Look closely. Feel it. These are carvings. They mean something!"

"I don't see anything."

"One end burnt. Some bumps here and there. "

"No, no!" Grandpa was almost frantic. "Can't you feel it?" He took the stick and rested it lightly in his palm. He closed his hand over it gently, staring intently. Closing his eyes, he concentrated deeply. In a long silence, he seemed to hold his breath, keeping in his excitement.

He opened his eyes, now wet with tears, and looked around at the men. He held up the stick.

"It speaks to me," he said softly. "It's the Memory Stick. I'm sure of it!"

"How could that be?" Uncle-Q asked. He turned to Cousin-Q and asked where he found it.

"There—in the grass."

The stick was sent around again for all to examine. With growing conviction, they began to agree with Grandpa.

"Yes it could be."

"It must be—"

They asked each other, "How?"

How could it be there "All this time?"

How did it get there —"Lost when they were driven here by the flood."

"It must have followed them from the Wash!"

"Resting there, waiting to be found."

By this time, Cousin-Q and others came to the group. The momentous news that the long-lost Memory Stick was found was quickly spreading, and more came with excited demands.

"Make it sing, Grandpa!" someone shouted eagerly. "Make it sing!"

Grandpa was surprised and taken aback by the idea of the Memory Stick singing there and then, on the spur of the moment. The Memory Stick always told its stories in a sacred ceremony.

"You can't sit down and make it sing just like that," he said. "Besides, I need to listen. It has much to tell me..."

He held the stick protectively. "It has been a long time. Now, this day, it was ready to come back to us."

Grandpa managed to move away by himself.

"Not now, folks," Uncle-Q announced. "Let's leave Grandpa alone with the stick for a while."

"The way things are," Old Quaymon said, "we may never hear the Memory Stick."

Cousin-Q demanded to know: "Why can't we? Why not?"

"It doesn't work that way," Uncle-Q said. "In the old days, they would have a grand ceremony. There, in the green country, before our people moved here, they always were under the stars for the Memory Stick ceremony. So when you heard the story of the Hero Stars, you could look up and see them, and understand what the Memory Stick had to say."

"That's what I meant," Old Quaymon said. "This place isn't good for that. It's too dangerous to be out during the dark. It's not the kind of place where you can have a real ceremony."

"Maybe someday," Uncle-Q consoled. "Not today, for sure. Don't bother Grandpa about it anymore."

Grandpa found a place in the shade. He could be seen leaning over the stick, touching it carefully, reverently, and listening, listening. Those who passed by said that they could hear a soft singing or humming. Was it Grandpa, or the Memory Stick singing? They weren't sure, but it was beautiful. They kept an eye on him, watching and waiting and hoping.

When Little-Q heard Uncle-Q say that only "someday" would they hear the Memory Stick, he knew it meant either "forever" in the future or "never." He went away dejectedly on his own. He found himself walking slowly down the path where he had gone with Papa-Q the day he'd left to scout a new land for the covey.

He looked longingly down the path. He felt an unease that he could not quite identify. "Just makes me sad to come here, I guess," he thought.

The feeling was brushed aside by his thought of the Memory Stick. "I saw it! I held it!" he realized. "Yes! I was there when the Memory Stick came back!"

As he moseyed along, the strange feeling returned. He decided that a snack would make it go away. Covey people seldom came down the path this far, so he had a choice of what he would like to eat. Ah! A juicy grasshopper.

"Good!"

As he browsed, he heard Mockingbird and Grackle squabble about who would have the highest branch in the tall cottonwood across the way beside the water.

They're always fussing with each other," he thought, looking up. It was then that he noticed that the sky was more open here than he remembered. "There aren't many big trees anymore."

Little-Q became so engrossed with the display in the tree that he did not notice Cat slinking in the tall grass. Mockingbird was no match for Grackle's size and long sharp beak. He fluttered away slowly in a manner that would show the white patches of his feathers, flying to another tree. This tree was not nearly as big, but Mockingbird pretended it was. He balanced on the thin, swaying topmost branches, singing his own song, letting everyone know he was there.

On the ground, Cat was lying in wait, watching Little-Q. Not far away.

Grackle, his point made, gave a loud "Grack!" and looked at Little-Q with an expression which said, "I guess I showed him—and you!"

Cat was stalking closer. Closer. Closer.

Little-Q raised his head to swallow another snack. Halfway through this movement he saw out of the corner of his eye a dark shape that did not fit into the pattern of scrub and grass and weeds.

Just as he realized "CAT!" the shadow came at him, moving silently, swiftly.

He looked for cover. "Dummy!" he scolded himself. "So busy eating and gawking..."

Too late!

He forgot his first lessons of having cover in mind whenever he was in the open. To always be alert.

"Always! Always! Always! his memory heard his mother scold.

He ran. As fast as he could. Not fast enough to outrun Cat. He lifted his wings. He flew a few feet. It was not enough to make a difference.

Without looking, he sensed that Cat ran toward him with great leaps.

Cat now was right behind him.

Cat was ready to make a final pounce.

One more jump—!

CHAPTER 10

Little-Q dove into the best cover he saw at that moment. It was a little patch of weed. But it was something. His breath came in frightened gasps. He made himself as small as he could. He kept absolutely still. He expected the worst. 'I hope it doesn't hurt too much.'

A long moment. He waited for the sharp claws of Cat in his back. Instead, he heard the sound of rapidly-moving wings. Very near. He heard the rush of a bird diving close to the earth. Feathers flapped noisily. He heard Cat squeal in surprise and hurt.

He heard Cat leap away. A crash, then a rustling, running in the grass. Little-Q heard more diving and flapping of wings. He sensed that Cat was gone. Driven away by—

He heard Mockingbird's voice: "You can come out now, little one."

Little-Q carefully backed out of his little bit of shelter. He turned and saw Mockingbird smooth his feathers calmly, trying to look modest yet proud of his feat.

"You—you saved my life!" Little Q exclaimed.

Mockingbird fluttered into the air far enough to show his feathers. Show the white.

Little-Q went on: "You dived on Cat and drove him away! That was a Hero thing to do!"

"Glad to," Mockingbird said. "Any time."

Grackle came down. With a grand flourish, he proclaimed: "Amazing! Wonderful!"

He talked as loud and braggy as if he made the rescue.

Mockingbird went into a long fluttering spin, showing his white feathers. As soon as he was off the ground, Grackle approached Little-Q with a serious expression.

"What do you think—didn't I tell you so?" he said.

"You've said so many things—" Little-Q said.

Grackle croaked a big "Grack!"—louder than usual–that made Little-Q flinch. "Doomed! Didn't I tell you? Didn't it happen?"

Mockingbird joined them. "Take it easy on the kid. Hasn't he had enough excitement for one day? Wasn't it enough that he was rescued from Cat? Rescued by a very skilled flier, while others watched."

Grackle was not put off. "That's over. The question is, what's next for this young man and his people?" He turned back to Little-Q: "You are certainly overcrowded where you are. Yes, I can see you down there. I suppose nerves are on edge. Everyone wants to move."

He turned with a great sweep of his tail feathers. He raised his beak and spoke to the distance. "I happen to know of a place..."

He started to pace up and down, looking important as he turned this way and that.

"Some people have talked about that," Little-Q said. "Moving, I mean."

"Yes, yes, of course," Grackle declaimed. "I can tell you of a wonderful place. Not too far..."

He looked Little-Q up and down and spoke again: "Not too far for those like us." He didn't say, "Fliers like us." Little-Q knew what he meant when he added: "You could do it, perhaps. When you know the way, you could guide your people."

"Wait! Don't listen to him," Mockingbird interrupted. "I have seen a place, too. The one I know about is just right for you folks."

Grackle raised himself up and glinted his beady eye at Mockingbird. "I fly to the highest places and I know the perfect land for his people."

Mockingbird gave a little twirl: "I fly higher and I know one even more perfect."

Little-Q looked from Grackle to Mockingbird. "Why don't you both just tell me where these places are, and I will go look for myself. "

"This most beautiful meadow is so nice and secluded," Grackle, said, "I doubt that you could ever find it on your own."

"Beautiful meadow?" Mockingbird put in. "Not as beautiful as the one I am thinking of. It's beyond the trail..."

"Yes, so is mine," Grackle said with some surprise. "Yes, beyond the trail."

"I can't go that far," Little-Q said. "No one in our covey can go beyond the end of the trail. Except for people like Papa."

Grackle wanted to know why.

"It goes to the end of the world," Little-Q said with a tremor of unease in his voice. "Papa went and—"

Little-Q ended with a sob he couldn't control. Grackle and Mockingbird looked at each other over his back.

"Perhaps if we all went together," Mockingbird said quietly.

"Yes, we'll all go together," Grackle said in an agreeable tone he seldom used.

Little-Q thought, 'Papa! Maybe I'll see Papa!' He raised his head and said, "Yes! I'll go!"

They set out together, Little-Q on the ground and Mockingbird and Grackle taking turns showing him the way.

As they neared the end of the trail, Little-Q noticed the Day-Star in the distance.

Mockingbird and Grackle argued from time to time about who was guiding and where they were going. The two fussed with each other so much, it made Little-Q nervous. If he had remembered the Day-Star he could have guided on that and come without these two busybodies.

The trail became less and less of a trail and more and more a mass of long grass and weeds.

Then they were beyond the end of the trail. Little-Q was in a wilderness—unexplored territory far beyond the Covey lands. He felt queasy. Grackle and Mockingbird encouraged him and there was the Day-Star and as they went on, he found that 'Yes! I can do it!'

After what seemed a very long time he came to a great dark place, which went under the ground for a distance. Little-Q stopped. This was too much. Mockingbird and Grackle came to him. They said he must go alone into this place.

"We'll see you on the other side," Mockingbird said.

"Is there another side?" Little-Q asked.

"Yes," Grackle assured him. "It's not all that far."

With much foreboding, Little-Q entered the darkness. Inside there was no sun. The cover, far overhead, made a great roaring sound all the time. It was the kind of ominous sound Little-Q was taught to avoid. He stopped partway through, ready to turn back.

"You've got to!" he told himself. "Papa may be right there on the other side."

It was not as dark as the darkness when we went with Grandpa, but it was darker than he liked. He went on, farther into the dark. He walked slowly, carefully.

The dark place went under the ground for a long space. Little-Q guessed it was about as far as the path from the nesting ground to the stables.

After he had been in the dark a long time, he felt brave enough to look up. He saw an opening. A few more steps and he saw Grackle and Mockingbird. Beyond them, the Day-Star.

They called to him and he went toward the light.

After the darkness of this place, he saw the sky. Below, land opened in a great green expanse. Yes, there behind Grackle and Mockingbird was a beautiful meadow. It sloped downward toward the land to the south.

This was not like the Covey land, which was dry and with few grassy areas.

Here was a great green meadow. Yes, with trees and, beyond, there was the Day-Star, closer than he had ever seen it before.

"It's beautiful!" Little-Q said. "So big! So green! Everyone will want to live here!"

Mockingbird gave his little flying twirl. "I was sure you would like my meadow. It's perfect for you people who—"

Grackle interrupted with a great noise. "Your meadow! This is my meadow and I am the one who guided him. It is I who has saved his people, and you would do well young man to keep that in mind."

Mockingbird noticed Little-Q's expression and asked, "What is it, little one?"

Little-Q looked away. His eyes were getting wet. Tears.

"Well..." Grackle said.

"I don't see Papa," Little-Q said.

He didn't see Grackle and Mockingbird look at each other and shake their heads.

Mockingbird did not want to give Little-Q the bad news of his doubts, so he said something vague. "I would guess he has gone into the land beyond..."

Little-Q brightened. "Is there a land beyond?" he asked.

"Yes, of course," Grackle assured him. "Up there—up that slope."

Mockingbird went on: "If you go to the top, you'll see there's more land."

That would be beyond the Day-Star! Little-Q said, "We would never go there."

"Why not?" Grackle asked.

"You've come this far," Mockingbird said.

"It's the end of the world," Little-Q said.

All right, then. This place is nice enough, isn't it?" Grackle suggested.

"Yes," Mockingbird put in, "you don't need to go beyond, do you?"

"No. I think this would be just fine," Little-Q said, and he began thinking about where the Covey families would live in this green expanse. Yes, tall grass there, and those old Palo Verdes over there, and there must be a lot to eat...

"What do you think?" Grackle asked.

"It's beautiful here," Little-Q said. "Thank you so much."

Mockingbird flipped his tail feathers sharply.

Little-Q quickly added: "Thank you both so much."

Little-Q noticed that the Day-Star was not as bright now and shadows were beginning on the far edge of the meadow.

"I'd better be getting back," he said.

"Yes," Grackle said, "your mother will be wondering about you."

"Worried about him," corrected Mockingbird.

"It's not that. Now that I've seen the meadow, I think I should get back home."

Grackle and Mockingbird had a lively discussion about Little-Q finding his way back. It went on almost as long as it took Little-Q to trot back through the dark space, past the wilderness area to the place where he could make out the trail back to Covey lands. The two birds flew off and continued their debate at the top of a tree.

When he came back to the Covey, Little-Q was puffed up. He had been gone quite a long time and done something quite special. He went to the end of the world and found a beautiful meadow! He was surprised and let down when he found that no one missed him.

He saw Quinata. She was in a hurry and said something about his games. He was too surprised to think of anything to say right away.

"Games!" he thought. "No! I've been scouting new land for the Covey."

Before he could to tell her, she went on. He kicked the dirt. He turned to watch her. She looked back at him. She smiled. It was a different smile than before, and that helped.

Even his mother! All she said was, "There you are! Grandpa has been looking for you to help with something. I think he might be up at the Pole."

When Little-Q came to the Pole, Grandpa was rummaging about in a patch of weeds and grass. He looked up and said, "There you are! Come help me with something important."

As Little-Q joined him, he said, "I've been looking all over for you. Where have you been?"

Little-Q began to tell him about his conversation with Grackle and Mockingbird and what they said about the Covey being doomed and they knew...

"Yes, yes," Grandpa interrupted, half-listening. He was busy searching for something near the place where they hid the Marking Stick.

"They told me about a beautiful meadow," Little-Q went on.

"I wouldn't pay too much attention to them," Grandpa said.

"They are so flighty. Always flapping about, making a lot of noise, poking their beaks into other people's business."

"They..." Grandpa looked up at Little-Q. "They don't understand what we do. Don't seem to want to learn. No respect for the work, I say. Yet, it's not something we can talk about, is it? So perhaps they don't realize, don't really know what we do. Do you suppose that's it?"

Little-Q decided that he would wait until later to tell his news about the meadow. Now he wanted to help.

"I've been thinking about our situation here," Grandpa-Q said, going back to his search. "It seems to me that we are not long for this place. We are too crowded. Nerves are on edge. We have no idea what might come next. We must be ready for anything."

"What are you looking for?"

Grandpa said he was looking for a really nice piece of wood which he recovered from a felled cottonwood a long time before: "The one by the water that was so special. You remember, don't you?"

"Grandpa, I wasn't born yet," Little-Q said.

"We used to have so many of those big trees. They keep taking them away. Now there are hardly any..."

He instructed Little-Q to stay beside him, so they could close the space and be more likely to find what he was looking for.

"When they were taking them away," he went on, "I found a beautiful piece from the roots of one of the very old trees. It was perfect for something special. I wasn't sure just what at the time. Perhaps the tree spoke to me and said, 'Take me and save me for when you need me for something important.' Now, I have an idea for something important."

Grandpa-Q moved abruptly in the tall grass, reached down and held up a piece of wood. "Look! Look! This it!"

He carefully ran his hands over it, feeling, testing, hefting. "Yes! This is it!"

He carried it to the Tall Pole.

"Your grandmother has spoken to me about saving things, but you see how fine this is?"

Little-Q ran after him. "What are we going to do?"

"The Memory Stick gave me an idea," he said. He walked around the Great Stone and with growing excitement explained his idea.

"Think of where we are today, practically pushed off our land. What if we are given another push? Will we be able to come to the Great Stone as we need to?"

"I don't think so," Little-Q said. "It's sometimes hard to get here now."

"Yes," Grandpa went on. "There's another thing: We certainly cannot move the Great Stone and take it with us. And we cannot remember all of its markings, can we?"

"Not me. There are so many marks."

Grandpa held the stick high, as if offering it up to Mr. Sun. Did he say something? Did Little-Q hear, "Thank you"? He knew that something important had happened.

Grandpa's hand moved as though the stick was quivering in his grip.

"We are going to make a stick that remembers the Great Stone!"

He handed the piece of wood to Little-Q.

Little-Q hefted it, felt it up and down, and held it firmly.

"What do you think?" Grandpa asked.

"It is nice."

"Nice! It is special! Very special. Let it speak to you."

Little-Q loosened his hold and the wood seemed to almost float in his easier grasp. He looked down at the wood. "Yes! It's doing something."

"Something special," Grandpa said.

"Yes, I can feel it." Little-Q handed the wood back.

"Think of it!" Grandpa said. "Just as the Memory Stick knows the story of our Covey back to ancient times, this stick will know about the marks on the Great Stone. If we ever need to move again, we can take that knowing with us."

They went into the shade and studied the stick. Grandpa said it would take work to do what he had in mind, but it could be done.

"We can do it," he said, turning the stick over and over, studying its root lines.

"Thank you, tree," he said, "for being here for us when we need you."

He went to store the new stick in the place where they kept the Marking Stick.

"That's good for today. Let's go look at the Memory Stick."

CHAPTER 11

Grandpa and Little-Q went back to Uncle-Q's place. Most everyone had their afternoon feed and were loafing and napping, as best they could, considering the crowd and the noise.

There was much grumbling and even grousing about the situation. Everyone seemed to be on top of everyone else.

"I feel like a prisoner," one mother said. "Living inside this fence is not a natural way for our people."

"Look at it the way Aunt-Q does: The fence that keeps us in is the fence that keeps Cat and his friends out. We sleep without worrying."

"Yes, I would agree with that. But the noise–that constant humming and the crash of the water! It's like living under a waterfall."

"Aunt-Q says you get used to it after a while and you don't notice it at all."

Little-Q ran into the midst of the covey and roused the young ones. "Grandpa is going to read the Memory Stick!"

"No, no," Grandpa-Q corrected. "Things are not right for a Memory Stick ceremony. Not now."

When he got the Stick, the young ones crowded around. They wanted to touch it. After cautioning them to "Be careful!" he let them, one by one.

There were questions about how it got burnt. Grandpa said it was a long story. They made a big to-do, begging for the story, disturbing the whole place.

Grandma-Q made a suggestion: "It's part of our history. Why don't you tell them." She looked over the heads of the young ones who were making such a fuss and added: "If you go out into the shade—over there—" she indicated a place outside Uncle-Q's—" it might be nice for all of us to have a story."

Grandpa nodded. "I understand." He led the young ones out and a little distance away.

He held the stick and rubbed it gently. There was a certain fondness and reverence in the way he handled the wood, which connected him with the Covey's tradition and history.

One of the young ones asked if the burnt part of the stick told the story.

Grandpa said, "No, the story of the burning is not on the Memory Stick in the usual way. But the burnt part does make us remember. That's what the Memory Stick is for."

He began to tell them how the Memory Stick was burned.

At that time, the Covey people lived on a land much like this. It was friendlier than the cold in the north. The Covey moved from time to time, but remained faithful to the Work by making ways to continue at each new place.

Their life was peaceful and happy, until one dark day. Invaders came without warning and with an awful force. They destroyed homes and scattered the people.

It was the first time the Covey people had seen the creature that came to be called Horse. So big. So tall. Such large feet. Feet that could trample a Covey person without Horse realizing what was under his foot.

There was no reason to the invasion and destruction. After a time, the invaders moved on. Disappeared. Perhaps they were on their migration.

But while they were on the land—so much damage!

When the invaders ravaged the nesting ground, everyone had to run for their life. They went in every direction.

As the dark approached, the Covey people came together on a small rise. They were away from the invaders but able to see them and what they were doing. Our people thought they would be safe during the time of darkness. Not many things move about in the darkness, you know. They kept watch.

Even after the dark came, the invaders had circles of light. The Covey people guessed that the invaders had captured the fire of the lightning. It gave them a very hot light. Even so, the invaders approached very close to these places of fire. Dangerous and barbaric! The Covey people had never seen such a thing.

The invaders were friendly with this fire and kept going back to it. They actually fed the fire itself. They brought pieces of trees they found nearby. As they needed more food for the fire, they brought new things. They took homes and other covey things from the nesting grounds to the fire. Finally, to the people's shocked dismay, the invaders found the Memory Stick and brought it to the fire.

One of them seemed impressed by the Memory Stick and looked at it and touched it. Perhaps he was more sensitive than the others. Finally he threw the Memory Stick into the fire.

He was careless and only part of the stick went into the flames.

Watching in awful dread, the Covey people thought the Memory Stick was lost. Their heritage and sacred memories were being fed to the fire to be eaten up by the hot bright flames. The history of generations of Covey people would soon be gone. They watched in helpless horror.

Suddenly a little shape ran out of the Covey.

"Someone about your size, Cousin-Q," Grandpa said.

Little-Q thought, 'Me! Me! Me!' and it showed.

Grandpa noticed and added: "Yes. Or you, Little-Q."

This brave member of the Q-Covey ran down the hill and into the invader's camp. He went right up to the fire. He grasped the end of the Memory Stick that was not in the flames.

He pulled and pulled. The invaders were blinded to what was going on as he worked to free the blazing stick from the flames. In a final, super effort, he was given the strength he needed. He pulled. Once more! There! The stick came loose.

He managed to get the Memory Stick to the slope. Brave ones rushed down and pushed the fire away with their wings. More came and helped bring the stick up to the Covey.

The Memory Stick was cloudy with smoke and very hot. The rescuer was exhausted and suffered bad burns. But he saved the Memory Stick.

"This," Grandpa-Q said, "is that same Memory Stick, handed down through the generations."

He let the crowd of young ones handle the stick. They were silent as they passed it around.

After a few minutes, someone asked, "Who was it, Grandpa? Was it you?"

"No, no" he said. "It was long before my time. It was one of our people. Perhaps your great-great-grandfather. One of our Hero guides, don't you think?"

Before anyone could answer, a small truck pulled up in the space between Uncle-Q's and Grandpa's story group.

This was not the color of the poison butterfly. It was white, like one they had seen around the horses from time to time. A man got out of the truck, the kind of man they had seen at the stables.

Grandpa gave the alarm. The group froze in full alert. But the ones at Uncle-Q's went on with their loafing and talking. Because of the noise, they were not aware of the danger.

Grandpa rose up, disregarding the hazard of becoming exposed. "Why don't they do something?" he said.

"They can't hear!" Little-Q shouted. "They can't hear the alarm!"

Little-Q began to run toward the nesting ground. Cousin-Q joined him. Both ran calling out the alarm.

The intruder stopped and looked at them. At this, they flew away from the covey in the classic defense maneuver to lure the intruder away from the people.

The intruder did not follow. He entered Uncle-Q's place. He kicked gently at something in the tall grass. "Git along little dogie."

Grandpa and the young ones watched as the man moved about, checking here and there. He approached the great noisy waterfall. His arms and hands moved.

Somehow, his motions made the roaring hum stop. At the same time, the waterfall stopped flowing. Abruptly, the place was silent.

The man moved about a little more, went outside the fence, and got into his little white truck. It went away.

"All clear!" sounded across the land. The Covey relaxed. The silence was so great; they could hear the sound of their breathing.

Uncle-Q shouted: "What was that all about?"

Then everyone had a question or comment. The place was abuzz.

One of the elders announced: "We'd better have a meeting and talk about this."

Grandpa sighed.

Little-Q and Cousin-Q made their way back to Uncle-Q's place. They were having a grand time, congratulating each other on how they saved the covey.

"Will that get on the Memory Stick?" Cousin-Q wondered.

"Maybe we will go down in history as heroes of the covey."

Mama-Q was not light-hearted about their feat: "What a crazy thing to do—!"

Grandma-Q was more forgiving: "If they hadn't given the alarm, there was no telling what would have happened."

Uncle-Q started to talk in the shout he used when there was so much noise. He stopped and began again in a softer voice: "That fellow didn't mean us any harm. In fact, he made the noise go away. Maybe it will be easier now for this crowd to live together. "

Grandpa called to Little-Q.

"Come. We need to go back and get started with our work."

Little-Q looked over at Cousin-Q and saw he and Quinata were talking. It looked like she was making a fuss over him. Or was he making a fuss over her?

Little-Q felt a quinge of jealousy. He thought, "If she knew what I was doing, she'd pay attention!" He knew it was something he could not talk about.

Little-Q followed Grandpa to the Tall Pole. He helped Grandpa set up the Calendar Stick and learned how it was to be used. Grandpa cautioned him that this would take a lot of time and he was counting on Little-Q to stay with the Work.

"So much depends on it, you know," he said.

"I will, Grandpa, but I don't understand why," Little-Q asked. "Why do we do these things?"

Grandpa-Q was taken aback and pondered a moment. "Why of course," he said. "You haven't—"

"No, I haven't."

"There hasn't been time. Everything has been so confused."

Without saying the words, both understood that ordinarily Little-Q and others his age would hear the story at the ceremony where they would learn the traditions of the Covey people and receive their names.

"The way things are going," Grandpa said, "I don't see when or how it can be done. Perhaps we can talk about it as we work."

He looked out at the Old Man of the Mountain, bright in the afternoon sun, remembering.

"I can't give you all the details that are on the Memory Stick, but I can tell you the important parts. You see..."

His session with the Memory Stick and the young ones—perhaps just touching it—put Grandpa in a story-telling mood. As he and Little-Q worked around the Pole, Grandpa pointed out this feature and that line and occasionally pointed to the Old Man of the Mountain and recounted how the Covey people came to the Work.

It was a story of the light and the dark. Order and chaos. Goodness and evil.

When things began, there was order and brightness. But something went wrong and the dark intruded. Where the dark came, there was chaos. They found that the dark was just over the edge and if given an opportunity it would get in and infect everything. Like the water that came down the Wash and got into everything and drove the people away.

Qwa-Qira-Ta saw what was happening with what he created and instructed the people to stop the dark. To do this, they must summon the light, which will turn back the dark. The call is most effective when the darkness is at its worst. Only by working at it constantly can the light prevail.

Qwa-Qira-Ta called on everyone to do this. The Covey people responded. Other people may have done, but it was easy to see that they soon became weak and gave into the dark. Others lost their belief or were simply lazy. From what followed, it appears that we are the only ones who have been faithful and strong enough to stay with the Work. All the others gave up.

Grandpa stood and stretched an ache out of his back. Little-Q was worried. Grandpa was moving more slowly these days. Grandpa, he realized, was getting old. Well, he was always old. Now, he moved old. Was he sick with something? Little-Q wondered.

"Even today," Grandpa went on, "we see invaders come with evil intent and bring chaos. They want to drive us out and away from the Tall Pole and the Great Stone. One of the insidious things about the dark is that it uses the elements of chaos and fear to try to weaken us and make the Work come to an end. Our ancestors promised, and we must continue the Work, no matter what. The world is depending on us and what we do. That's why we must find ways to keep the Work going.

He seemed to cheer up with a remembrance: "We have moved before—and the Work goes on!"

"Yes," Little-Q said. "Didn't we move here from the Wash? I wonder, did we have a Tall Pole there?"

"Yes, of course," Grandpa said. "They worked with that Pole for a long time, and were able to bring most of its marks here by sheer memory. I don't think I could do that."

"This time we will have the Calendar Stick, won't we?"

"Yes. If we move again, we will have the Calendar Stick."

As they finished up, Grandpa-Q said, "One more thing..."

"Yes?" From Grandpa's tone of voice, Little-Q knew he was going to say something very important.

"I probably don't need to say this, but just to be certain..."

He stopped on the path and faced Little-Q.

"The ancient ones taught that the Work keeps its strength when it is not dissipated, that is, not made common. If spread thin, it will lose its energy and it will not be effective against the dark."

Grandpa went on: "Even your friends Grackle and Mockingbird and Sparrow do not understand. I would not try to convince them—or even discuss the Work with them. What they will do is try to dissuade you, weaken you. I don't think that would be good for the Work—or, for that matter, for the whole world."

"All right," Little-Q assured him. "I understand."

CHAPTER 12

The covey settled in at Uncle-Q's place. With the new-found quiet, tempers softened. Gleaning the remains of the stable and corral provided food for all. The weather was cooler, disturbed only by an occasional afternoon thunderstorm.

Grandpa and Little-Q worked steadily on the Calendar Stick. Little-Q wondered why they hurried so. Working on the stick with Grandpa made him miss some of the best games. He noticed that Quinata was beginning to take part. Cousin-Q seemed to spend a lot of time consoling her about the loss of her mother and father and others of their covey.

Grandpa pressed ahead with unusual urgency. Grandma-Q remarked on how he pushed himself, and Mama-Q said she was worried about him.

"He just doesn't seem his old feisty self lately," Mama said. "But he goes at this like he has to finish before—before something happens." "Being Qwa-Say-Qua is a big responsibility," Grandma said. "Everybody has forgotten about that thing which came in here and made the water stop. It may be back for something else one of these days. Those things are not to be trusted, you know."

One day, Grandpa announced that it was time for a Memory Stick story. He would read the Stick during the quiet time between the afternoon feeding and the coming of the darkness.

Before then, he wanted to spend some time alone with the Memory Stick.

This meant that Little-Q was free to play with his friends. Everyone was there and at first the running and kicking games were great fun. Soon, he and Quinata were bickering with each other. She knew rules which they played by in the land to the north. These were often different from the rules Little-Q was used to. There were constant arguments about what was right.

Cousin-Q acted as peacemaker. He told them that they were spoiling the games for everybody and to stop their arguing for a while.

Complaining about "Girls!" Little-Q agreed.

Shaking her head and saying, "Boys!" Quinata also agreed.

Finally, they settled on the traditional game of Run-Q-Run, which was played the same in both Coveys. Little-Q liked this game and went at it with a zest that had been quashed a long time.

Once, when Quinata was the seeker, he thought he found the perfect hiding place.

Sparrow gave him away and she found him right off. She laughed at him all the way back.

Then Little-Q was the seeker. He found most of the hiders. He could not find Quinata. No one had seen her. After everyone looked everywhere, they decided it was going beyond being a game and began to worry.

Little-Q had an idea about where she might be. He went to the place where he first saw Quinata. From there worked his way north.

The trail was hardly visible, since most of it was covered over by the marauding monsters. He kept with it, and found her at the far side of the covey land.

Little-Q saw her, standing alone and still, looking toward the land to the north. She seemed to be humming, singing a plaintive song. One he was not familiar with. He suddenly felt saddened.

She sensed someone was there and turned.

"You found me," she said quietly. "You win the game."

"No game this time," he said. "I thought you might be here."

She came toward him.

"I don't understand."

"Sometimes I do something like this," he said.

"Go off by yourself, you mean?" she said.

There was a softness and kindness in her expression. This was the first time they were alone and close and speaking like this. Each able to see the other and begin to understand what they felt.

"Sometimes," he said, "I go to the trail where you can see the Day Star and the end of the world. That's where Papa left to scout a new place for us."

"Is that the place you showed me?" she asked.

"Yes, I go there and wonder when Papa will be back," Little-Q said.

"Now that I understand, it will be special for me, too."

"We're all sad that Papa's been gone so long. My mother especially. I'd like Papa to come back and make her smile again. I know the old people talk about Papa now and then but they always stop when I come around."

He was surprised that he talked so much and told this girl his deepest feelings. He hoped she wouldn't make fun of him.

"I think I understand," she said. "It must be hard waiting and not knowing."

"But you—" he thought of Quinata losing her family. "I'm sorry. You've had it worse."

"It's been different for me. It's all over for me now."

He almost said, "Don't worry —I will take care of you!" because that was the way he felt, but the words came out: "We will take care of you."

She shook her head. "You may have to move some day."

"I know a meadow," Little-Q said. "It's a beautiful meadow—out there, almost to the Day Star. You will go with us."

They heard a voice, "Who's there?"

It was Sparrow, busy in his little tub-shaped depression in the ground.

"Must you disturb me, wherever I am?" Sparrow scolded.

"Sorry," Little-Q said. "I was here with Quinata. Have you met Quinata?"

"Yes—that girl from the north. Hello there."

"Sparrow keeps telling me things will work out," Little-Q told her.

"Don't worry," Sparrow said. "There are so many places to go. Always new places."

"Yes, I suppose so..."

Sparrow shook dust through his wings. "The old man doesn't look too good lately."

"He's been working really hard," Little-Q said. "I guess he's tired."

"Perhaps it's the weather. It affects the old ones." Sparrow glanced at a large bank of clouds forming over the mountains. "We may in for a bad spell one of these days."

"What makes you think so?"

"See the way those clouds are shaped? They have been doing that every afternoon. That's always a sign of something big coming on. We think it's a sign of heavy water."

Sparrow fluffed the dust out of his feathers, squiggled his tail and flew away.

Watching him go, Little-Q saw the angle of the sun. "We'd better get back!"

Grandpa-Q found a place in the sun for the Memory Stick story. He said the warmth felt good on his back.

"We weren't always people of this land," Grandpa said. "A long time ago our people lived far to the North. There were tall trees and grassy meadows and cool streams. Peaceful. A friendly land. It must have been wonderful to live there.

"Then something happened."

He rubbed the stick reverently, listening, listening.

After a time of closeness with the Memory Stick, Grandpa began the story. It was like the Stick spoke its memory through Grandpa.

Qwa-Qira-Ta kept a close watch and the Q-people lived well for a long time.

Then little by little something upset the order of things. They wondered many times what they did to bring it on. The cold came and stayed.

The cold got into everything, even when Mr. Sun was high overhead. There was much suffering because of the cold.

The people began talking about moving to another place. The elders warned that any new place they moved to could be as bad or even worse. At least where they were they had memories of good times and it was always possible that the warmth and the good times would return—in the next season, perhaps.

The cold and the suffering continued. The elders met again and debated a long time. They decided they really did not have a sign that this was the end of their stay on these old grounds or that it was time to move on.

Besides, they said, where would we go? What direction would we take?

There came a morning which was like no other morning. Mr. Sun gave only a dim, hazy, cold light that was frightening in how it made things look.

Then it began. The cold fell from the sky. It took the form of tiny white feathers—so soft, so beautiful, they tempted the people to touch them. But they were oh, so cold! They stuck to everything. Every thing. Soon the ground was covered, so that their feet disappeared into the tiny white feathers. So thick and so deep and so cold that the people couldn't find food or water. Everyone began thinking, "This looks like the end of us," and a few grumblers said it right out loud.

Qwa-Say-Qua tried to give them hope. He got up on a tall stump and got their attention. It hurt to look up into the cold to see him.

Mr. Sun is angry, he said. I will go again to the Tall Pole. I'll try to reason with him. Even if he doesn't listen, this time must pass, and beyond this there has got to be a better time. We must be strong. Stronger than the cold.

There they were, the proud Q-Covey reduced to a pitiful clutch, huddled in the cold, one body shivering against another. Qwa-Say-Qua went to the pole and was there all day.

When he came back, cold and shivering, he was silent. He just shook his head and they understood. The people didn't know what to expect. That night, their fate came on them. There was a mighty rush of cold wind, so violent it woke everyone from their sleep.

"The sky is falling!" someone shouted.

The people went out from their shelters to see what was happening.

The clouds were gone. In the cold, everything was crystal clear.

What the people saw was so astounding it was written on the Memory Stick as the Night of Falling Stars. It changed our history.

The stars fell—in brilliant streaks which lighted up the whole sky. The trails of light made it almost as bright as day, but without warmth.

The falling went on and on.

The streaks of fire from so many falling stars made light enough for Qwa-Say-Qua to go the Pole.

He raised his wings and stretched his feathers to the utmost. He cried out.

When he did so, a great warm wind came across the land. Yes! This time a warm wind.

It came from the edge of the world. It seemed to come directly out of a beautiful pattern of very bright stars.

He knew that this was the answer we were waiting for. He went back to the Covey and found that the people had felt the warm wind and seen the star pattern.

They were wondering what it meant.

An old one who knew the old stories—stories so old they were not written on the Memory Stick —said that the star pattern was very special to the Q-Covey.

"That's Hero-Q!" she shouted. "He lives in the sky now. He was our guide in the old days, when we moved at night.

"You lazy people," she scolded, "you have gotten so weak in this place, you have forgotten our heritage."

The people agreed that what they saw was very special. So bright and well-formed. Steady in the sky. Something to guide on. Was it a sign to move?

"Yes," Qwa-Say-Qua said. "I am sure it is a good sign for us. It is beckoning to us."

Some hesitated and wanted the elders to meet, but he said they should act immediately.

"This is our sign," he said, "We are going to follow. I'm sure it will lead us to better things."

So the Covey people left their homes and started out. They followed as far as they could that night. Little by little the air became warmer, the soil softer. The cold stopped its awful biting. They could reach the ground for food, and they found water.

Just as Qwa-Say-Qua said—everything was better.

The people followed until they fell, exhausted. They slept, awakening only to eat, and then to sleep again. By the time of darkness they were rested and refreshed, and they followed the guide stars once again.

This went on for many times. There were many hazards, many rivers to cross, strange lands to pass over, but Hero-Q guided our people to the warmth.

Finally one day they awoke in a place much like this–and found it good for them at that time.

Realizing that the story of the night of falling stars was ended, the children clamored for more. Grandpa said, "No more. That one is enough to ponder for a while."

Quinata looked at Little-Q and smiled.

"You know a meadow." she said. "Perhaps you will guide us one day."

"Yes!" Little-Q thought. "Like Hero-Q!"

He looked at her smile. Was this a tease or was she serious, he wondered.

CHAPTER 13

It was a dark, cold, confusing day. Of a sudden, disaster fell on the covey. The people could not understood why, and blamed themselves. What did they do wrong? They searched for reasons but found no explanation.

The calamity began at first light. The cold made it worse.

The dark had been bone-chilling cold, which came on quickly and unexpectedly. When light came, it made the world an eerie blanched color. There was no sky. Only an awful cold cover that held no hope for warmth.

The small white machine came with several of the standing-up people. They entered Uncle-Q's place and began broad sweeping movements. Big back-and-forth sweeps which were overpowering and devastating. They cut down the grassland and destroyed the covey homes.

The protection that kept Cat out now worked against the covey people. They were pushed around—herded like horses.

The first sweeps quickly forced many out of the place. As the sweeping went on, more and more were driven out, crying in terror and anguish. They huddled along the trail.

As far away as the Tall Pole, where they were finishing their work, Grandpa-Q and Little-Q heard the cries.

"Listen!" Little-Q said. "Another attack!"

"They need help," Grandpa said. "You go. I'll finish up here. I'll come right away."

Little-Q found chaos. The elders, stunned by the sudden attack, were as confused as the rest and did not know what to do.

"Where's Grandpa?" they shouted.

"He's still at the Pole," Little-Q told them. "He'll be here as soon as he can."

The air was filled with terrified questions: "Where will we go? What can we do?"

Quinata saw him and shouted: "Do something! You've got to do something!"

"What can we do? There are too many of them and they are so big! "

"You know a place! You said—"

Little-Q thought: "That was just talk. This is real."

Out loud, he said, "That was different."

"Your people need help now and I don't see anyone else doing anything. You've got to!"

Grandpa arrived and the people crowded around him, crying out and shouting. Someone asked about Papa-Q and his scouting report. What happened to that?

"He is not back yet," Grandpa said.

"If not Papa-Q, then who?"

"We have to do something now."

Another shouted, "Where can we go? Who can show us?"

"We have to go," Grandpa said. "We have to get to a new place and—" he looked up at the deadly pallor of the sky "—do it quickly. We've got to—-"

"Little-Q knows a place!" Quinata shouted.

"No, not me," Little-Q groaned. "Not all these people depending on me."

"He knows the way to a beautiful meadow!"

Others took up the idea:

"We have to move, Little-Q!"

"Show us the place!"

"Don't make me!" Little-Q thought. "It's too important."

Grandpa clapped him on the shoulder. "It looks like you are our only hope!"

Grandpa quickly organized the move. Little-Q will lead. The elders will make sure everyone stays together. Cousin-Q will guard the rear.

As Grandpa was giving orders, Mama-Q saw what was happening with Little-Q and came to him. In a motherly gesture, she put her wing around him as best she could. This was not easy because of his size now. She spoke softly, privately.

"You can do it," she said. "Remember, you have the stuff of heroes. Just be steady and do what you have to do."

Grandpa-Q gave a last glance around at what little remained at Uncle-Q's place and told Cousin-Q: "It looks like we are finished here. Don't leave anyone behind."

To Little-Q he said, "Guide them to this beautiful meadow. I will stay with the Pole. Come back as soon as you can."

With a reluctant heart, Little-Q started out. The people crowded onto the trail to follow. Once underway, he looked back. He was surprised to see all the covey people following him.

"Following me!" he thought. He immediately had second thoughts: "Can I do this without messing up?"

As they went, the weather worsened. A cold wind. Drizzle turning into freezing rain.

Even so, the move was going well and Little-Q was encouraged. "Maybe I can do it!"

As the trail became less of a trail and more overgrown with brush and grass and weeds, the trek became slower. The rain made it miserable.

Little-Q was confident, because now he could see the Day Star, far away in the rain. He used it to guide on and pressed forward.

After a time, he felt a quiet and looked back. The people had stopped where the trail withered away and disappeared.

He hurried back. "What is it?" he said. "Come on!"

"This is the end of our land," one said.

"Yes, we aren't permitted to go beyond the trail."

"But we must," Little-Q said.

"We are at the end of the world."

"No! No! This is the way Papa went," Little-Q assured them.

"Yes, and he hasn't come back!" was the reply.

One of the elders came up, and asked, "What's the problem?"

"We are at the end of the world."

"We cannot go on."

He looked around and turned to Little-Q. "They are right. This is nowhere. You want to take us beyond the end of the world?"

"It's all right," Little-Q said. "Look—" he pointed to the Day Star— "I am guiding on the Day Star—you can see it there. The end of the world is beyond that. The meadow comes first."

Another elder heard this and said, "He may be right." His feathers shivered under the freezing rain. "We can't stay here, that's for sure."

Quinata came up. "You've got to get these people out of this awful rain. Stop talking and do something!"

Everyone talked at once, telling her why they stopped. Quinata interrupted: "I've seen a sky like this in the north and I know it's going to get worse. The people need cover. Some trees or bushes or a patch of sage. Anything!"

Little-Q remembered the way under the noise that led to the opening onto the meadow.

"Yes!" he said. "I know a place!"

Without thinking, he shouted, "Follow me!"

He turned and set off, guiding on the Day Star.

He looked back. They were following him. Now he was leading! Dashing his enthusiasm just as quickly were the first fallings of the tiny cold feathers that stuck to everything and made everything they touched feel freezing.

He hurried on.

In time, they reached the opening, which went under the earth and opened onto the meadow. But the falling of the cold feathers cut off any view of the meadow. The covey huddled in the dark under the noise and waited for something to happen.

"It's got to get better than this," someone said.

"That awful noise!" another complained.

After a time, the covey settled down, huddling together for warmth.

Mama-Q came to Little-Q. "You look exhausted. You'd better rest."

"I've got to get back to Grandpa," he said. "It has taken so long."

"He will be all right for a while. Rest a bit. Get your strength back."

"Just for a minute," he said.

Little-Q eased into her warmth and was quickly asleep.

Little-Q awoke with a start. "It's been too long," he said. "I've got to get to Grandpa."

He quietly left the covey in the shelter.

Outside, the dark was not as intense as he was used to when he went to the Pole for the Work. He was late!

Did Grandpa start without him? He began to run.

He marveled at what had happened to the land. The white feathers were no longer falling. So many had come down to the land they now covered everything. The air was unusually still.

He realized that the dim light was from the struggle beyond the Old Man of the Mountain. It reflected off the cold white things that were everywhere.

Somehow, for all the cold, the world was beautiful and peaceful. Even the devastation at Uncle-Q's place looked serene with its cover of the cold white.

He hurried on. At the Tall Pole he found that the Great Stone was covered by the white feathers. Except at one edge, where a bit was brushed aside, as if by a wingtip.

And there— "No, no!" he heard himself cry out–was Grandpa, lying on the ground. The tiny white feathers stuck to him. He was so still! "It's my fault! I should have been here!"

In his horror, Little-Q could not move. He raised his wings and heard himself cry out. With a voice louder and more impassioned than he had ever had in his whole life, his anguish echoed off the Old Man of the Mountain.

At that instant, a brilliant shaft of light struck his eye. Very quickly, the light from Mr. Sun spread across the land. The cold white feathers reflected Mr. Sun's brightness with a dazzling brilliance that made Little-Q's eyes hurt.

He heard a voice. "What is it? What has happened?" He turned. Grandpa was struggling to get up from the ground. Little-Q hurried to him.

"Grandpa! Are you all right?"

Grandpa shook the white stuff off his body. "Yes, yes, I think so."

"What happened?"

"I pushed some of these cold things off the Great Stone. Then I turned and must have stumbled. I'm all right now."

Little-Q was not so sure. He looked closely at Grandpa. Is he getting too old for the Work? he wondered.

Mr. Sun warmed Grandpa and he explained. "What happened was, I went to check the Great Stone." He looked around, wonderingly. "Mr. Sun is so bright now. So warm..."

He asked what Little-Q did. "Tell me exactly what happened."

"I'm not sure," Little-Q said. "All I did was—when I saw you, I guess I yelled. Without thinking about it or anything, I just yelled—"

Grandpa was silent for a moment, absorbing this information. Quietly, he said: "You have the gift! You will save the covey!"

Little-Q did not understand and did not have time to ask.

Grandpa asked how the Covey move went. Little-Q explained where the people were sheltered during the dark, and with the coming of the light they would see the entrance to the beautiful meadow.

"You had no trouble finding it, even in that awful weather?" Grandpa asked.

"I guided on the Day Star," Little-Q said.

"Yes, of course!" Grandpa said. "The Day Star! I know it well. In fact, I've been thinking..."

He walked around the pole, brushing off the cold.

"We are not long for this place," he said. "The Pole may be the next to be destroyed. These things never let up. We must move the Pole."

"Move the Pole?" Little-Q asked. "How? We are nothing compared to the Tall Pole or the Great Stone."

"No, not the Pole itself. Or the Stone. We will move the knowledge of the Pole and the Stone."

Grandpa held up the Calendar Stick. "With this, we have what we need to carry on the Work."

"Yes, but—" Little-Q said. "Where?"

Grandpa held up the stick: "Let's see where Mr. Sun leads us. Perhaps to the Day Star, near the end of the world."

CHAPTER 14

Grandpa and Little-Q came down from the Tall Pole and, guiding on the Day Star, went to the opening under the ground where the covey people had taken cover.

The sky was bright, the air cold.

As they trotted down the trail and across the wild, they found that the tiny white feathers, which covered everything, were turning to bits of water in the warmth of Mr. Sun.

"Look, Grandpa," Little-Q said, "the little white things are disappearing from everywhere. What does it mean?"

"Yes, that's their nature. You don't see them very often, and when they do fall from the sky, they don't last."

"Maybe we should be sure to mark this on the Memory Stick."

"Yes, that's something to consider," Grandpa agreed. "We've had unusual fallings from the sky lately. I wonder if something has gone wrong. I'm afraid I'm losing my strength and that's what has brought on these strange and unusual events."

"No, Grandpa!" Little-Q objected. "Everyone is depending on you."

Little-Q heard Grandpa mutter a "Yes, yes.." followed by musings so quiet he could hear only a few phrases.

"I've been talking with the elders ...the Work after me ..if Papa is not here ..you are the only one of your family..."

"What did he say?" Little-Q thought. "Does he mean me? I couldn't do that! I might. I could try. But alone? Maybe if Cousin-Q helped..."

At the opening under the earth, they found that the covey people had gone out into the light. They were scattered to various places of the meadow, making new homes. Some looked for a friendly tree. Others preferred to make a home under a thick bush. A few went the old way and made a nest on the ground, but near cover.

Grandpa and Little-Q went through the meadow, up the hill beyond and over the water to the Day Star. Grandpa walked around the pole of the Day Star. He brushed off dirt and dust that had accumulated on the stone at its base.

"Yes," he said, "This will be fine."

Little-Q looked at the stone and saw faded markings on it.

"Looks like someone has been here before us. That's funny—these look like our markings."

"Yes," Grandpa said, "people of our covey were here a long time ago. My grandfather and people before him. When I was very young, he brought me here and showed me the work that was done before the flood drove them away. It was quite an adventure to come this far from our home with the horses."

He shrugged off the memories with a "Let's get to work" gesture. He wanted to make sure that everything would be ready when they came to the pole in the dark.

"We will dedicate this as the new Pole," he said. "Then the people will be more comfortable in their new homes."

Grandpa directed Little-Q to locate the cache for the marking stick. He had a recollection of a safe, secure place that they used in the old days. A place they would keep secure to safeguard the Work.

"Try over there," he suggested. "It will be just like the one we had near the place of the horses."

Little-Q went to look. Grandpa worked with the Calendar Stick, scribing its memory onto the stone at the base of the pole of the Day Star.

The silent intensity of his work was interrupted when Little-Q came running. He called out: "Look, Grandpa, Look!"

"What is it?" Grandpa asked. His tone gave the message, "What is it that is so important to interrupt what I'm doing?"

"A feather! Look! I found the cache place and there was this feather!"

Immediately interested in his find, Grandpa took it and carefully turned it this way and that. "One of our people, don't you think? Not from the old days. This came here not too long ago. "

"Yes, oh, yes!" Little-Q exclaimed.

Grandpa studied the feather again. "How?" he wondered. He asked Little-Q to show him where he found it. Grandpa made a close examination of the area.

They went back to the Pole.

"Can it be—?" Little-Q exclaimed.

"Hush, hush," Grandpa cautioned as he turned the feather over, held it up to the sky, blew on it gently. After a long moment, he said, "Tell me what you have in mind about this feather."

"I think—I know!—that Papa was here. He left his feather to tell us that he was here. That he is all right, and he went on to scout far lands for the Covey. That he is safe. That we will see him again. That—oh! I've got to tell Mama!"

Little-Q could hardly hold his excitement as he watched Grandpa, who was gazing at the feather as if his mind was reaching beyond today's events.

"What is it?" Little-Q asked. "What do you think?"

"I think you are right," Grandpa said. "Your mother will want to know right away. This feather says something important."

He handed the feather to Little-Q. "Go, now, and show your mother."

Little-Q started to run off.

Grandpa called to him: "Little-Q—ask her what it means."

Little-Q ran to his mother. At first his excited manner made her anxious.

"What has happened?" she asked.

He held up the feather for her to see, and she brightened: "What is it?" she asked

"Look, Mommy, look!" he said, handing it to her.

She held it softly. "Do you know where this came from?" she asked.

"I found it up at the Day Star where Grandpa is setting up the new pole," he said quickly.

"No, I mean, do you know whose feather this is—who left it there?"

"Yes! Yes!" Little-Q exclaimed. "It's Papa's feather! I know it. I just know it. Grandpa thinks so too."

"Yes, I am sure of it. That means—"

"Papa was here!" he went on. "He left this feather as a sign. Papa was here!"

"Perhaps we will see him soon," Mama-Q said. "Let us keep this in a safe place as a token of that promise."

"Grandpa said to ask you what it means. What finding this feather means."

"Yes, son," she said seriously. "This feather has another message."

She put her wing around him as best she could and went on:

"When you were first out of your egg, your grandpa said he had been given a name for you. I have wanted to tell you that name. The time has never been quite right. You know that your name must remain secret.

"Yes," he answered seriously. After a moment he whispered, "What is my name?"

"The name given to you is Strong Feather. Just like this one which your father left. He meant for you to find it, I'm sure."

Little-Q touched the feather reverently and whispered the name to himself. "Strong Feather. I am Strong Feather!"

"Good!" she said. "You must live by that and all that it means."

Little-Q remained quiet, listening to her words, his heart thumping with excitement. He had anxious questions. What does it mean, really?

Before he could ask, his mother went on: "You see, a feather is very light and supple, but very strong. It protects you when the water falls from the sky. It comforts you with warmth in the cold dark. It is strong for those times when you fly. The colors show the world who you are —who your covey people are. When you are still, your feathers hide you. When you have children, the feather makes a nest soft to hold the egg. When they are out of the egg, your feathers wrap around them to show that you love them. When you raise up your wings to protect them from danger, the feathers show your bravery."

Little-Q sighed, burdened by the seriousness of it all.

After a moment of silence, she asked, "Does that help? Do you understand?"

"Yes, " he said, "I am Strong Feather."

Mama-Q gave him a hug: "My Strong Feather!"

When the time was right, Grandpa called for the Pole ceremony, and all the people gathered together for the dedication. The event quickly became a festive celebration, which even a growing cloudiness could not mar.

Uncle-Q again demonstrated the strutting-booming-puffing-dances of the distant north country relatives. The rhythm and movements were so exciting that others joined in. Old Quaymon was one of the first.

Little-Q and Cousin-Q jumped up to join the circle of dancers. He was surprised to find himself opposite Quinata. They hit it off in a way that made Little-Q feel good and he noticed that she seemed to be having a good time, too.

Grandpa stood up and started to go into the circle. Grandma tried to stop him.

"Sit down!" she scolded. "You're too old for this sort of thing."

He pulled away and pointed at Old Quaymon. "If he can do it, I can too. Just watch!"

The dancing became more vigorous and as it went on, Uncle-Q dropped out. Old Quaymon, too. Grandpa was caught up in the rhythm and continued the dance movements.

Suddenly, he stopped, breathing hard. He wavered and clutched his breast. His face showed intense pain. He turned to leave the circle of dancers. He collapsed to the ground. Grandma was watching. She ran to him, screaming. Others went. Soon the scene in the meadow showed two distraught groups. The men huddled around Grandpa and the women gathered around Grandma.

After a time, Old Quaymon came out of the group of men. He looked over at the women. Grandma stared anxiously. He shook his head in sad finality.

At that moment, the sky fell.

In the downpour of water, some of the men stayed with Grandpa. Everyone else went to the shelter of the opening under the earth.

Grandma stood looking out at the water falling on the meadow and wept.

"You see," she said, "even the sky weeps for Grandpa."

Later, Old Quaymon took Little-Q aside. "Your Grandpa said he had been given a name for you."

"Yes, Mama told me," Little-Q said.

"Good! Grandpa said it was a strong name, and just right for you. You must live by that. I'm sorry we cannot have a naming ceremony for you and the other young ones. There are so many who have missed the old things, because of all this moving around."

Little-Q did not know what to say.

Quaymon went on, "Grandpa also said you are to carry on the Work."

Little-Q thought. "Not me!"

"I'm not sure—" he said.

"Grandpa said he had been watching you grow up. With Papa-Q gone, you are the one."

Little-Q was aghast. 'Me! Alone at the Pole! Helping Grandpa was one thing, but doing what Grandpa did —I could never do that!'

"I have just helped..."

"Grandpa said you talked to Mr. Sun. He said you did a remarkable thing that day."

"Alone at the Pole—"

"The elders want you to have help and so we have designated someone to go to the Pole with you."

Little-Q immediately thought of Cousin-Q. Yes, of course! They could work together.

"You mean someone like Cousin-Q?" he asked.

"No, the elders were thinking of someone else," Quaymon said. "They selected one of those who came to us from the north. Her name is Quinata."

"Quinata?" Little-Q asked.

"Yes. Her father was head of that covey," Quaymon said.

Little-Q said, "Yes, I understand."

He said the words. Inside, he was not so sure.

"Quinata!" he thought. "She is the one who made fun of his children's games. Now she had seen him dancing and having a good time. What does she think of that?"

Quaymon touched his shoulder with a gesture of encouragement. "This is what Grandpa wanted. You must start in the next darkness. She will go with you, of course."

The place where the Covey was sheltered under the earth became brighter. Outside, Mr. Sun had overcome the falling water.

They heard Grandma call— "Look!"—and hurried to where she was standing at the opening onto the meadow. A span of many colors curved across the sky with luminescent brightness.

"What a sign!" Grandma said.

Mama-Q came to her side. "Perhaps it will help dry your tears."

CHAPTER 15

Little-Q went to the Pole with foreboding mixed with anticipation. The evening before, Mama-Q told him, "Don't worry, son. You will not be alone. You will have strength and support. Perhaps a sign will reassure you."

Quinata met him partway and followed in the dark. Neither spoke as they crossed the meadow, went up the hill and over the water to the Pole.

At the Pole, she spoke softly, hurriedly, because of the dark.

"I know this is your first time without Qwa-Say-Qua," she said. "I feel your anxiety and share it. But we were chosen and we must do what needs to be done. Old Quaymon told me that all the elders agreed that you have a strong spirit and will do well."

Little-Q thought, "I hope they are right."

He told Quinata where the marking stick was stashed. He went to the Pole. Anxious worry soaked his whole being.

"What am I doing here?" he wondered. "I'm not like Grandpa. This is so important, and I am not worthy."

Quinata called softly: "I have the Marking Stick."

"Good," he answered.

His thoughts were otherwise: "Someone better than me should be here doing this. I could make the mark on the stone when Grandpa was at the Pole. But now..."

He peered into the darkness. "I must try!" he told himself. "Concentrate!"

Making an intense effort, he saw in the far distance the jagged outline of the Old Man of the Mountain and the struggle going on behind him.

He felt Quinata approach and turned with a tinge of irritation. She interfered with his concentration.

"What is it?" he asked.

"I thought you would want to see this," she said, holding out something. He could not see it clearly in the dark.

He thought, 'What could be so important to interrupt the work we're here for?'

He came down to her. She handed it to him. He peered at it, and recognized it more from feeling than seeing.

A feather! It couldn't be Papa's feather. He gave that to Mama. "Grandpa!" he thought. "But when?"

"A feather," Little-Q said softly.

"Yes," she said. "A strong feather. I can feel it."

A shiver went through him. He felt stronger, yet at the same time sad. Grandpa is missing this first time at the new Pole.

"We'd better get to work," he said.

Little-Q went again to his post, as he had seen Grandpa do so many times at the old Pole. He gazed out toward the Old Man of the Mountain, who was guarding the edge of the world.

As he stood there, suddenly a great grief from all the events of days past swept over him.

He lifted his wings, holding the feather high, in a display of anguish. His bearing expressed a deeply felt sorrow and appeal.

He cried out.

At that instant, a blinding streak of light struck him full in the face. It came through a v-shaped opening in the side of the Old Man of the Mountain and slowly spread its brilliance and warmth over the land.

When Little-Q and Quinata came down from the Pole, they found Aunt-Q cornered by Grackle, who was pacing to and fro, making his loud "Grack!" noises.

She called to Little-Q and Quinata for help.

"Make this awful bird go away!" she cried. "He keeps telling me the most terrible things!"

Little-Q told her not to be frightened. "It's just his way."

Quinata sympathized with Aunt-Q and said Grackle did the same thing to her when she first came to the covey.

Aunt-Q was so upset she could hardly speak. "He told me—he told me—"

Grackle swept back and forth, making grand gestures with his broad tail and throwing his sharp beak around.

"I merely told her," he said, "that this place where you have settled is—what do you people call it?—the Wash? She said, Oh, no! This is your beautiful meadow. I was ready to debate the issue when she started screaming. Very irregular for a debate. Very."

"Yes," Little-Q spoke up. "That's what you and Mockingbird told me when you showed me the way. A beautiful meadow."

"Yes, of course. I won't deny that. But—"

Little-Q gestured across the green expanse. "Look— don't you think this is the most beautiful meadow you have ever seen?"

"I may have mentioned a beautiful meadow," Grackle said.

"You wanted a beautiful meadow, and here you are. It is merely a matter of the terminology you are using at that moment."

"If this is the Wash," Aunt-Q said, "I'm not staying. My grandmother told me about the terrible flood."

"Terminology," Grackle insisted.

"What do you mean?" Little-Q asked.

Aunt-Q's sobs interrupted. "Our people were almost swept away in the flood and they lost everything. This is no place for my family. We're clearing out!"

Quinata went to Aunt-Q and comforted her.

Grackle made a dramatic sweep. "A Wash. A beautiful meadow."

Quinata turned to confront Grackle: "What is it exactly that you are talking about?"

"May I offer the thought," Grackle said, "that they are one and the same–that your beautiful meadow is in the middle of the Wash?"

He emphasized his point with a loud "Grack!" and flew away.

Aunt-Q turned on Little-Q: "Look what you've done! You and your beautiful meadow! You brought us here—to the middle of the Wash!"

Later, she told Uncle-Q and he suggested that the elders have a meeting and discuss the matter. They agreed that what Grackle said about the meadow being in the Wash was a possibility. In the matter of the flood, they referred to the Memory Stick, which told them the flood came from rushing waters, which followed a fall of water from the sky so great it could not be counted.

The elders decided that since there had not been a great fall of water from the sky for a time and there was none of the rushing water that came with the flood, the covey would be all right for now whether they were in the Wash or in a beautiful meadow.

"Besides," as Old Quaymon put it, "even if we wanted to leave, where would we go? We seem to be very close to the end of the world."

In the days that followed, as Little-Q and Quinata worked together at the Pole, he found that he acquired more insight into what was going on, and became more and more enthusiastic. It was no longer a chore of going out into the dark and helping. He found a mission in the Work itself.

One day, he realized he was ordering Quinata around, just as Grandpa had directed him. He apologized.

"It's all right," she said." I want to help any way I can. I want to learn."

He was embarrassed. "I don't know what I can teach you," he said. With a spirit which surprised himself, he added: "But I am learning."

He walked around the stone, studying the marks Quinata made.

"Yes, I think we are doing very well."

"What does it all mean?" she asked.

"Look at these marks. You see, Mr. Sun rolls up and down the Old Man of the Mountain. Back and forth, like an egg rolling on the ground. See here!" He pointed to the Stone. "When Papa made this mark, it was very hot. When I made this mark, it was not so hot. Now, look here, at your mark—"

"You mean when the mark is here, Mr. Sun is very hot, and when it is over here..."

"Yes. The way he goes back and forth has given me an idea..."

"Yes," she encouraged him. "I want to learn. Tell me."

"I'm not sure I should even talk about it. It may be one of the secrets of the stone."

"Yes?"

He took the marking stick and walked around the stone, pointing here and there.

"You remember the old people on the Memory Stick who endured times of very cold. Our people here have times of very hot. You see these marks of Mr. Sun rolling from cold to hot and back again."

With growing excitement, he went on: "It seems to me that we could find a place from Mr. Sun between the very cold and the very hot and settle him there. Every day would be just right. Not very cold and not very hot. Wouldn't that be wonderful for the whole world?"

Quinata shook her head seriously. "I'm not sure that is a good idea."

"Don't you see," he said impatiently, "it would never be too cold or too hot. Everything would be just right all the time."

"One of our old stories told about the one who upset the natural order of things and it affected the whole world. Maybe you've heard it. It was the day of two suns."

"Yes! Grandpa said there was a story like that in our Memory Stick! How could you have heart it?"

"Our people had a Memory Stick too. It was lost when we were attacked. I can see now that the story was meant to be a caution to us."

"Grandpa said that it was one of the stories we lost when our Memory Stick was put in the fire. What was it about?"

"One day this fellow began ordering Mr. Sun around to suit himself. Mr. Sun became angry. He just stopped. Right where he was. He went dark and the whole world went dark. It was only by the work of everyone at once that Mr. Sun showed himself again. It came to be known as the day of two suns. The story taught us to be very careful to upset the natural order of things."

"You may be right. Perhaps we'd better be careful."

"You should be careful," she cautioned pointedly. She went on in a gentler, convincing tone: "Have you considered that what we are doing is enough? Perhaps the world does not expect any more from us. That it is enough to come a do the Work. I think we should keep on with that and not try out other ideas."

Clearly disappointed, he said, "Yes, I suppose so."

"You must do more that suppose. You must promise."

Surprised at her insistence—her strength—he agreed: "you are right. We must not try to change the natural order of things."

"Good. That's settled," she said. "After all, the most important thing, is confronting the darkness, is it not?"

He was aghast.

"Yes, of course," he said softly,

One day, Little-Q and Quinata came from the Pole and crossed over the water to go down to the meadow. On the way, they saw Duck playing in a trickle of water that came into the meadow through an opening in the place that held the crossing-over water.

"Hello," Little-Q said, "I haven't seen you in a while. Have you been traveling?"

"Yes," Duck said. "It has been the most wonderful time. But, you know, travel is getting to be very tiring. There are fewer and fewer places to rest. It's really difficult to find a decent place to layover around here."

"I don't remember seeing water here before," Little-Q said.

"Poor Duck!" Quinata said. "That's just a trickle."

"You can get your feet wet. If you hunt around, the food can be pretty good. I thought that if I stayed a bit, this trickle might lead to something more interesting."

"What do you mean?" Little-Q asked.

"Sometimes trickles like this grow to become something really worthwhile—you know, just flood everything and turn out to be quite succulent as far as food goes."

"Flood? Did you say flood?"

"Yes, of course," Duck said. "We like an occasional flood, especially in land like this which is usually without good watering places."

CHAPTER 16

When rumors started that water was seeping into the meadow, the people were at first skeptical. Then word spread about Aunt-Q's confrontation with Grackle—that Grackle said their beautiful meadow was in the Wash. The two ideas were tied together, and the people became frightened. After all, everyone had an ancestor who had been driven out of the Wash by a flood.

Mothers went to the elders and demanded to know what was going on. They held an open meeting to discuss the matter and the options the covey might have if the rumors proved true.

Even as they talked, the trickle became a rivulet, which expanded and began to spread water more quickly across the meadow.

Someone called out: "It's flooding! We'd better get out of here!"

"Where can we go? Where is a safe place?"

Little-Q called out: "I know a place! "

He was thinking of the place of the Pole, which was on the rise above the meadow. The people would be safe there, he was sure.

Aunt-Q and others scoffed at him.

"Why follow him! He promised us a beautiful meadow and look where he got us!"

"Yes—he guided us right to the middle of the Wash!"

The water was getting worse.

Quinata saw what was happening and knew that something must be done quickly. She called out: "Follow me! I'll guide you! You'll be out of here and safe."

She glanced at Little-Q and he understood that she was thinking of the very same place: At the Pole above the meadow.

She began to run to the slope, and many people followed.

Some of the men waited, wanting to make one more point in their discussion, wanting to talk some more.

Old Quaymon watched Quinata and said, "She is taking them to the end of the world!"

"No," Little-Q assured him, "she's taking them up to the Pole. They'll be safe there."

Quaymon objected, "There's so little cover up there. Everyone will be exposed to danger."

One of the men said, "My feet are soaked. Let's talk about this later."

They all ran for it, following Quinata.

Quinata guided them up the slope, over the water and to the area of the Pole. The people were amazed at how far they could see from this higher place.

"Magnificent!" one said. "You can see all the way to the Old Man of the Mountain."

"The land here is so bare, so exposed," another objected. "This is not a natural place for us."

But when they looked back at the meadow and saw water everywhere now, the objections died away.

"Good thing we got out when we did."

"Yes—thanks to Quinata!"

168

The men stood around and studied the water flowing down the meadow. They speculated whether the water would run on through, leaving a beautiful meadow again.

"There is so much—you can't see the end of it!"

To calm the excitement, Quinata promised the people that she and Little-Q would give them tours of the Pole and explain the Great Stone.

"What we are doing helps everyone," she said, "and everyone in the Covey should know about it and share in it."

She told them to gather at the next loafing time. Meantime, she urged the people to find new places to live here on the higher ground.

Later, when the people gathered around the Pole, Little-Q and Quinata explained the work which Grandpa and Papa-Q did and how they were continuing the tradition.

Old Quaymon made a little speech, reminding the covey how important the Work was and that it must continue.

"The whole world is depending on us," he said.

Little-Q took Grandma-Q to the place of the cache, and showed her the Calendar Stick which Grandpa invented. He told her about the feather which Quinata found on their first visit to the new Pole, and how Quinata said it was a strong feather.

"I felt it, too," he said.

"I'm glad you found that," she said. "No one has ever known, but your grandfather's name was Strong Feather. After Papa left to scout, Grandpa chose you to help with the Work. Perhaps one day you will be our Qwa-Say-Qua. After your father, of course."

"Do you think Papa is all right, then?"

"Just a feeling I have," she said, touching her heart. "Here."

As they were talking, a white machine, similar to the one they saw at Uncle-Q's place, came on the land and stopped nearby. Then another and a third, which was larger.

The machines moved about the covey in a threatening, surrounding manner, which made everyone uncomfortable. Their discomfort soon grew to fright as they saw large devices unfurled.

They took cover as best they could in this place, which was high and exposed, as the Pole was meant to be. They could not understand what was happening.

Then a great thundering sound broke out. Everyone panicked. None of the usual defenses worked. Some tried to flyaway. Others ran.

The flyers were quickly grounded. They and the ones already on the ground found themselves running away from the pounding noise into a bright tunnel.

There was nowhere to go but forward, farther into the place. It led to a large container which was very dark. Darker than the opening under the earth which went to the meadow.

All of the covey people were herded into this dark enclosure. Frightened beyond anything they had ever known, they huddled together. There was nothing they could do.

Many strange noises. After a time, the container moved. They traveled a very long time.

When the container that held them came to a stop, the light had ended and the people were pushed out into the dark in a strange place.

Little-Q was surprised to find that he still grasped the Calendar Stick. He must have held it tight all through the ordeal. He wondered, 'Will I ever use this again?'

Exhausted from the travel, frightened for their lives, the people found themselves on the hard ground of desert. They stayed together for warmth.

Exhausted, Little-Q fell into a deep sleep.

He awoke with a start. He was warm. Incredibly, it was light.

"How can that be! But the Pole!"

He saw that Mr. Sun was everywhere.

Around him, people were rousing out of their sleep. As they moved about in this place, they found food on the ground—succulents and seeds, some their favorites—and plenty of water.

Little-Q couldn't believe it. 'What's going on?' he wondered. He saw Quinata in the distance. 'She must have done this!' he thought.

Quinata was talking with Mama-Q. The whole world turned upside down and they are chatting like old times!

Something momentous had happened and he was left out of it. He felt angry and hurt. Grasping the Calendar Stick, he ran toward them.

"What is it?" he called. "What's going on?"

Mama-Q welcomed him.

He confronted Quinata, shouting, "What have you done?"

Mama-Q told him to calm down. "Everything is all right."

Quinata smiled. "Let's take a walk and I'll show you."

She took him down a fence line. The covey people around them seemed safe. They went about their breakfast as if nothing had happened. They smiled at him! Greeted him!

As they walked together, she pointed out features of this new place. Old Palo Verdes. A large patch of tall grass perfect for nesting. There were plants he was not familiar with. Food was handy and in abundance. Water, just over there.

She led him toward a little rise. They followed a fence line for a time.

They turned a corner.

Down the fence, sitting on a fencepost at the top of the rise, head high and topknot silhouetted against the sky, was a figure which looked familiar. Beyond, Little-Q could see a pole. It was very much like the Day Star which was their Tall Pole above the meadow.

Little-Q ran, crying loudly, "Papa! Papa!"

Papa came down and he and Little-Q exchanged a tight hug. They were both so moved they could not speak.

Mama-Q soon joined them and everyone was talking at once. There was a lot of catching up to do, and the newcomers heard Papa's story.

Papa-Q made his way to this new place by guiding on the Hero Star.

"It seemed to be an ideal place for our people," he said, "but when I tried to return to bring the Covey, I could not get back. There are barriers, which I could not get through.

"I was forced to wait, hoping that somehow you folks would do the same—guide on the Hero Star and come to this place. I don't know how you did it, but here you are!"

Little-Q asked about the barriers and what that meant.

"I'm not sure what we can do about them. I'm going to talk to the elders about it."

Papa and Little-Q quickly became absorbed in discussion of the Work. Little-Q was glad that he was able to bring the Calendar Stick. They compared the information on the Stick with work Papa had been doing.

The two women smiled and walked away.

"They'll do fine," Quinata said. "The Work will continue."

"Yes," Mama-Q said, "but won't you be part of it?"

"It was exciting for a time. Now I feel it's time to settle down and begin a family."

Mama-Q remembered that the covey women were preparing for a festival and suggested they go over and get in on the planning.

"It's a beautiful time for a festival," Quinata said.

"Yes, I think the warming time after the long cold is the best of all."

Papa was impressed with the work on the Calendar Stick and asked how it was done. Little-Q explained how Grandpa started it and then both he and Quinata worked on it.

"This is excellent!" Papa said. "Do you suppose she would want to join us?"

"Yes, I've wondered about that. I'll ask her."

From the very first, the covey people found that life was easier in this new place. A small white machine, which was not hostile, would come every day and spend a little time on the land. After it left, the people found food. It was more food than they could eat, so others from the surrounding land joined them to eat and water.

There was a drawback to this comfortable life. The people began to realize that although they had good food and water and nesting places, they were more or less confined to this place because of the barriers.

The elders met and discussed the issue.

Some were happy living in this new place and did not question the situation. Others longed for the old open spaces where they could move when they wanted and go where they wanted.

"That didn't always work out the way we would have liked," someone said, reminding the group of the places that the Covey had to leave, usually in a hurried flight for survival.

"If we made it around or through the barriers—what then?" another said. "There's hardly any food out there and I haven't seen any water and there must be snakes and things. I think my family is safer in here than out there."

"Times change," someone else said. "Perhaps this is what is meant for us at this time."

The debate came to the question: Is this a natural way of life for Covey people? This caused more discussion, but they could not reach a decision.

Finally, Old Quaymon, who hadn't said much until then, got up and said:

"I don't know a lot about all the pro's and con's and in's and out's and feathers and fluff, but let me say this: I believe we are doing good just being here and doing the Work. Remember the whole world is depending on us. If we fly off and do something crazy—now, that could really upset the natural order of things and the whole kit and kaboodle would be gone—phht!—and we'd go with it."

There was more murmuring among the elders. They broke for lunch, and then loafing time, without a decision.

Little-Q felt guilty about hogging the Pole work and went to Quinata for a serious discussion about it.

It was noisy where she was and he asked what was going on.

"They're getting ready for a festival," she said. "The first at our new place."

He suggested they walk down the path by the fence line. On the way he apologized for ordering her around at the Pole.

She smiled, almost enjoying his discomfort.

"Not at all," she said. "I understand. I enjoyed the Work and getting to know you better."

"We've been talking—Papa and me—and we're wondering if you would want to join us at the Pole and take up the Work again."

"It was exciting, but that part of my life is over for now."

She looked at him seriously. "I think I would rather settle down and begin a family."

He hadn't thought of that.

"That is," she went on, "if anyone would have me."

"I'm sure—you're so attractive and smart and so likeable...well, more than likeable...you could have the pick of the covey."

"Do you think so?"

"I know Cousin-Q has had his eye on you for a long time."

"He's nice, but—" She hesitated a moment, giving him a searching sideways glance. "I don't think he is quite my type..."

"Oh, okay." Little-Q felt a surge of anticipation rise up in his chest. His heart began thumping faster. He heard the sounds of the festival in the distance.

Quinata smiled at him in a most attractive way.

"They're having a celebration," she said. "Why don't we walk over that way and see what's going on."

"All right," Little-Q said. "What kind of celebration is it?"

"I think it's a wedding festival. It's the season, you know. "

"All right," he said. He felt his heart thumping faster. A lump rose in his throat.

Little-Q and Quinata came into the festival area. A crowd of couples—everyone he had grown up with—was standing in front of the covey. When the newcomers arrived, everyone cheered. Little-Q heard shouts from the pals he played games with not too long ago.

In a moment, Little-Q and Quinata were with the other couples and pushed to the front of the group.

Cousin-Q, who was standing beside him with his girl, poked him in the side. "Everybody is looking at you," he whispered.

"Smile."

Suddenly, it was quiet. Little-Q felt everything go serious.

Papa-Q came and stood before the crowd of couples. He said a few words.

Quinata looked very seriously at Little-Q and he stared back. She said something. He nodded and heard himself say, "Yes."

Papa-Q finished. The whole covey cheered. The ceremony was over.

175

Cousin-Q poked him again. "Congratulations! Life goes on, hey, Little-Q?"

Little-Q smiled and poked him back. He thought, "I wish they would stop calling me Little-Q."

There were dances and refreshments long into the day. Later, Quinata and Little-Q went to look at nesting places and make plans for a home of their own.

Printed in the United States
64340LVS00002B/110